MW00571415

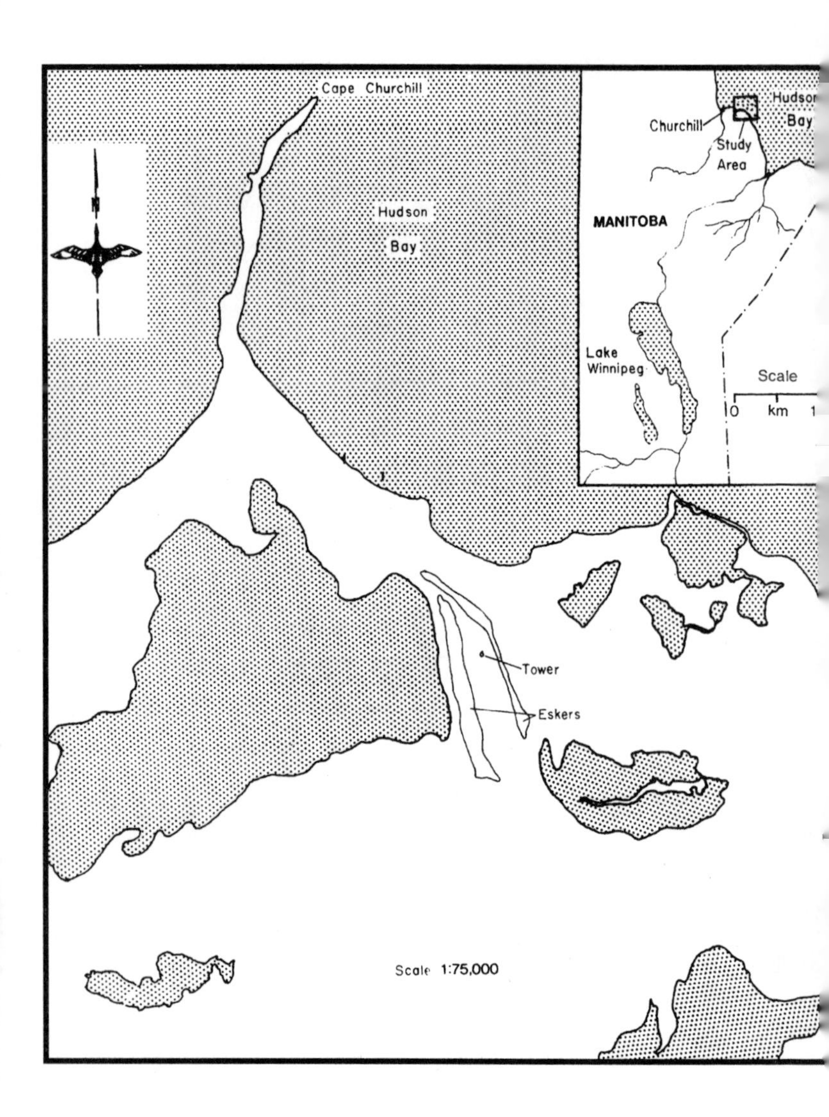
Cape Churchill
Hudson
Bay
Churchill
Study
Area
Hudson
Bay
MANITOBA
Lake
Winnipeg
Scale
0
km
Tower
Eskers
Scale 1:75,000

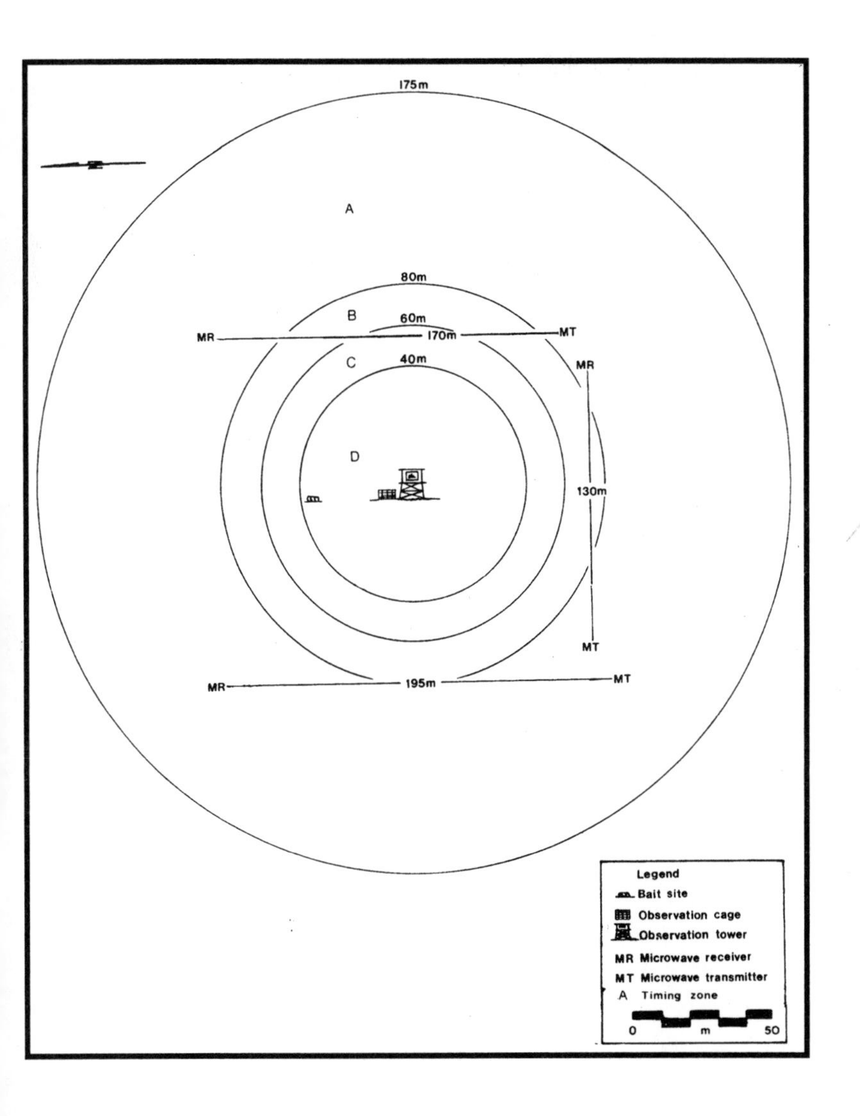
175m
A
80m
B
60m
MR
170m
MT
C
40m
MR
D
130m
MT
MR
195m
MT
Legend
Bait site
Observation cage
Observation tower
MR Microwave receiver
MT Microwave transmitter
A Timing zone
0
m
50

POLAR CIRCUS

POLAR Circus

by

D.A. BARRY

Polar Circus

published by Ravenstone
an imprint of Turnstone Press
607–100 Arthur Street
Artspace Building
Winnipeg, Manitoba
R3B 1H3 Canada
www.TurnstonePress.com

Turnstone Press gratefully acknowledges the assistance of the Canada Council for the Arts, the Manitoba Arts Council and the Government of Manitoba through the Book Publishing Industry Development Program for our publishing activities.

Canada

Original cover photograph by Trevor Bauer

Author photograph by Quaife/Rave

Interior photographs courtesy of L.R. Quaife

Maps reprinted by permission of Resources, Wildlife and Economic Development, Government of the Northwest Territories, from Northwest Territories, Dept. of Renewable Resources, *Bear Detection and Deterrent Study, Cape Churchill, Manitoba, 1982* (Yellowknife, 1983).

This book was printed and bound in Canada by Friesens for Turnstone Press.

Canadian Cataloguing in Publication Data

Barry, D. A. (Darlene Alice), 1948–
Polar circus

ISBN 0-88801-253-5

I. Title.
PS8553.A771685P64 2001 C813'.6 C2001-911102-9
PR9199.4.B37P64 2001

For Mistaya and Tanka

TABLE OF CONTENTS

ACKNOWLEDGEMENTS

That knowledge which stops at what it does not know is the highest knowledge.

—*Chuang Tzu*
The Music of Heaven & Earth

I would like to extend my gratitude to those people who shared their knowledge with me: Robert Bragg, Trevor Edwards, Terry Field, Catherine Ford, Art Glassford, Murray Laidlow, Percy and Lorna Lazdins, Chris McLachlan, Lesley MacDonald, Bernd Rave, Dereck Louw, Al Taylor, Tom Walker, and the librarians of the Calgary Public Library.

Special thanks to consultant and editor Ron Quaife, and to my friend Brenda Unger, who listened patiently as I told this story.

"The Curse-ed Ursid Blues" appears with permission of the Scatological Blues Band.

I am pleased to recognize The Canada Council for the Arts support for this project.

Without science, we should have no notion of equality;
without art, no notion of liberty.
—W.H. Auden

It is the marriage of the soul with Nature that makes
the intellect fruitful, and gives birth to imagination.
—Henry David Thoreau

The passion of justice is a primal embrace between
man and all his known universe.
—D. H. Lawrence

SCAVENGERS

THE SILENCE OF ROCK AND SNOW WAS SCARRED, not by a V-flock of Canada Geese beating hard over Hudson Bay, but by the unnatural wings of a helicopter. Rising in a way no bird does, the chopper lifted off from the polar bear research camp at Cape Churchill. The blades beat out a tattoo of urgency and dread.

The pilot, Conrad Cain, buzzed low over a patch of Ungava willows, surprising not bears, but ravens and Arctic foxes—the North's most relentless scavengers. Cain circled and set down near the black and white congregation that removed itself to watch.

Chuck Ford's clothes were scattered nearby, including what remained of his deflated eiderdown ski jacket.

"Oh, no. Oh, God, no." From the safe world of glass and metal, Allsun Skelly looked with horror at the tundra. If she was to remain in control of her wits, she knew she should not take her eyes off those wretched tatters of cloth. Allsun willed herself to see the scraps as prayer flags on the side of a Tibetan mountain. It was no good. She had to look, because she would have to act. Something would be expected of her.

Chuck's shredded clothes seemed more substantial than he, himself, did. There was little left. More than one starving bear had been here during the night.

Once Conrad had finished talking to the research camp by radio, he directed his attention to Allsun in the seat beside him. "We should document the site. You understand?" He waited for a nod. "I'll get your camera." He turned to Neal Casimir sitting behind them. "I've got some garbage bags. I think we should take him back."

This was it, what must be done. Allsun was relieved. She would do what she'd done for all her adult life: put a camera between her and the too real. Her sense of reprieve was tinged with guilt. How was Neal managing? A quick glance told her how hard this was for him. Rigid and pale, he stared at the birds hopping and flapping, dancing a little closer with bright, avid eyes alert to what remained.

Before she could speak, Conrad was back from the rear storage compartment with her camera and a shotgun. "I'll cover you while you take the pictures," he said.

There were puncture wounds on Chuck Ford's head and neck, the eyes were gone with the birds, the body opened and the cavity emptied, ribs apparent, most of the flesh torn away, muscle stripped from arms and legs, gleam of white bone in the gore. Allsun searched for the best angle, the right words to frame the unimaginable. Isolating and focusing through the camera, she was struck by the beauty—blood and bone against rock and sky, curves of white and gray shot with red.

Allsun returned to the men whose eyelashes and beards were already thick with ice. She stowed the camera in the helicopter out of the weather and took the

Winchester from Conrad. Hands freed, he pulled several green garbage bags from his pocket and handed one to Neal.

"Just one?" Neal asked.

"That's enough for his clothes."

"But—"

"I'll deal with the body. No need for both of us ... I've done it before." Conrad nodded at Neal. "It's okay."

Despite Conrad's attempt to spare Neal, he needed help prying away portions of Chuck's corpse frozen to the ground. When she wasn't scanning a land so open some thought it featureless, Allsun watched the men's faces, which appeared bleached—carved bone surrounded by parka hoods of fur and cloth—masks in a bizarre death ritual.

The land was calm, the birds incensed, the foxes curious. There was no scent of death in this frozen place, just the sound of metal scraping rock, ravens screaming and foxes nervously pacing. Blood on the overturned rocks resembled lichen, as if this starkly beautiful land had already begun to transform what remained of an individual life.

CAPE CHURCHILL
October 30, 1986

neal

He will look, but he won't see. He promises himself.

Kiss of life kiss of life kiss of . . . he focuses his seeing brain on this mantra, looks past the blood on Jane's lips and gets to work.

Everything falls apart: can't find her pulse, keeps missing the count . . .

Too cold. Cold to the touch. His hand frozen white against the red spectacle of her blood.

He looks on, loving her generosity . . . scarlet flowers blooming on the white snow around her. Such beauty to bestow on a land as inscrutable as its stone men.

Could it be she loves the Arctic more than she loves him? A new thought, an impossible act . . . because she is kissing him with a fully open, generous mouth . . .

Allsun

"NEAL. PLEASE, NEAL." Allsun covers Neal's mouth with her own and blows. His lungs rise on the rush of air. Counting off the five seconds, filling her own lungs, she bends to him once more, and again, and praying and breathing and counting. She cannot leave him to go for help. Screaming into the wind will do no good. Her isolation is complete, a necessity of nature, of this place.

His eyes flicker. "Neal," she calls. "Neal, wake up, open your eyes. Please," a whisper against his lips, as she seals her breath to him.

He is staring at her, calling her *Jane, oh Jane.*

In slow motion she moves back inside the Tundra Buggy, grabbing a sleeping bag off the nearest bunk to cover him.

His eyes are closed again. "No," she shouts. "Neal, no ..." Allsun presses the downy bag around him. Raising her hand, she slaps his cheek, hard.

His eyes fly open. "Allsun ..."

"Are you alright?"

"I'm ..."

"Keep your eyes open. Promise. I'll get the others. Just keep your eyes open."

Allsun charges over the gangplank, forgetting to do a safety check. Climbing the tower, suddenly she recognizes her own pain, driven into consciousness by the bite of frozen steel rungs on bare hands. She's nauseated. The nausea is a flood that weakens her grip on the tower ladder. Her legs shake, and for a sick moment she forgets she is twenty feet off the frozen, rocky tundra.

Her knees buckle. There is an airy feeling that makes her think she could fly. All she needs to do is push off and spread her arms. But first, she must warm her fingertips so she can stretch them to the stars. Releasing her grip, Allsun brings the fingers of one hand to her mouth, sucking all four. Replacing them on the steel rung, she feels a kind of burning. Reassured, the fingers of her other hand are bathed in wet warmth. Gripping the rung, she's ready to ascend. Allsun lifts a hand, ripping a strip of skin from each wetted finger. This new pain [illegible] cry out, "Help! Guy, help me!"

[illegible] wires anchoring the tower to this [illegible] earth mocks her, muttering away in the face of her plight like a cleric recording the proceedings of an Inquisition.

She knows now that the skin of the painless hand is also frozen to the tower rung. To lift it, to ascend, is to rip it raw.

Her own breathing reminds her of Neal. Allsun does not fly, but she makes the remaining twenty-five feet to the tower hut with martyred hands.

NEAL IS STARING at the sky—a blacked-out window, bits of paint scratched away, letting pinpricks of light through. He studies the patterns. He must be camping. He's out with Jane, doing fieldwork. Where is she? He wants to sleep. Promised Jane he wouldn't. Where is she? Why is he out in the cold?

GUY THORPE IS on his knees, his fingers pressed hard against Neal's carotid artery. He rips back the sleeping bag, pulls up Neal's shirt and puts his ear to Neal's chest. The heartbeat is irregular.

Jud Ash arrives on the Tundra Buggy deck with Allsun. "She shouldn't be out here," Jud grumbles at Guy.

Allsun had startled them when she threw open the tower hut door, appearing out of the night like a northern harpy in flannel shirt, long johns and lace-up moose hide moccasins. Her long red hair wildly tossed, it was clear she'd come from her bunk in the Tundra Buggy below.

Guy dressed as he tried to get Allsun to tell him what was wrong. She wasn't making any sense. All he knew was it had to do with Neal. He ordered Jud to stay with her. But when he made for the door, she would not be held back. Allsun fought Jud as if her life depended upon it. Neither of them was a match for her fury.

"Get a jacket on her and bring her down," Guy said.

Before Jud could object, Guy was gone.

A reluctant nursemaid, Jud helped her back down the tower ladder, her fingers bleeding into a pair of his woolen gloves.

"She shouldn't be out here," Jud repeats. "I think she's in shock."

When Guy doesn't answer, Jud wonders just what kind of camp manager Guy is. "Guy?"

Guy gives Jud a hard look. "Better down here than alone at the top of a forty-five-foot tower."

He turns to Allsun. "How'd he get out here?" Guy asks, shouting down the wind.

"Me . . ." Allsun is slumped on the deck beside Neal.

"Why?" Guy presses.

"I don't know." She hugs herself.

"You pulled him out?" Guy has one of Neal's hands between his own, rubbing it briskly. He nods at Jud to do the same with the other hand.

"Out . . . yes. I heard hissing." Allsun tries to look at Guy. Shakes her head. He's a blur.

Then he's gone. Inside the Tundra Buggy.

"No!" It's meant to be a shout, but there is only breath

before her eyes, frozen white fog. It must be there in her head . . . white fog . . . that's why she can't think. From the deck, the Tundra Buggy looms white in the darkness. A box trap. Vermin . . . trapping vermin on the ranch. The vision overwhelms her and she forgets that the Tundra Buggy is just an oversized white school bus on tractor tires. A bunkhouse with a deck at either end.

Guy returns, gloved hand covering his nose and mouth. "Propane. The furnace valve's leaking." He gulps clean, cold air. "We gotta move Neal."

"You don't mean up the tower?" Jud looks incredulous.

"No, across to the lab trailer." Guy bends, preparing to lift Neal under the arms.

"How will we get him down the hatch?" Jud takes Neal's legs, trying to hold the sleeping bag in place.

"Carefully," is all Guy says. Struggling against Neal's weight in his arms, he checks below the gangplank for polar bears, moving his head from side to side to throw the beam from his headlamp down along the ground. He backs across.

Jud follows, supporting Neal's lower body. He also trains his headlamp on the ground below.

"Allsun," Guy calls out. "Stay there. I'll come back for you."

She stands, trying to focus on the men. Sound makes them visible. Her eyes record sluggish shapes, her ears set the record straight. "Neal," she says into the white fog, "Neal."

Guy and Jud cross the plywood platform that has been constructed between the legs of the tower and lower Neal onto the roof of the lab trailer. Jud opens the hatch in the trailer roof and swings down in. A second later his head and shoulders appear in the opening, his arms guiding Neal's legs toward him. They maneuver Neal down the hatch.

To Allsun it looks like various white rabbits disappearing down a rabbit hole.

Then Guy is beside her, leading her across a white void. On the other side, she stops, caught in the updraft of light from the hatch.

Glancing up, Jud thinks she looks like a deer stunned by the headlights of an oncoming car. He helps her down, directing her feet toward the chair placed under the roof hatch. She's tall enough to barely need this makeshift stepladder.

Inside the lab trailer, Guy starts the propane heater. This one he checks first by passing his bare hand quickly over the valve, prepared to suffer a cold burn to his palm. Propane fuel is colorless, and when released from compression, rapidly expands, freezing skin so that it burns in response.

"Is he breathing?" Allsun asks. "He called me Jane …"

Guy's head snaps up to look at her. "What?"

"I gave him . . . you know," she puckers her lips and blows. "Can't think of the name … kiss of life …"

"You gave him AR?" Jud interjects.

"Had he stopped breathing?" Guy demands.

"I can't remember. I think so." Allsun has wedged herself in under the workbench, next to the heater. She is staring at the stains on the gloves Jud had put on her hands.

Guy directs his attention to Jud. "Do you know anything about propane poisoning?" He tries to calm his voice, take charge.

"No, not really. Do you?" Jud watches Guy, aware that he is struggling to maintain his role as leader now that his well-run camp is in crisis. Jud takes some satisfaction from this observation.

"Not this kind of thing. Not when it's been inhaled inside a closed room." Guy puts his ear to Neal's chest again. He knows of no first aid for these circumstances. Helpless, he can only monitor.

"Seen a barbecue cylinder explode," Jud says. Guy detects excitement in Jud's voice and wonders about his assistant.

"Yeah. I left both doors open on the Tundra Buggy." Guy notes that Neal's heartbeat is still irregular.

"Dead right."

Guy turns to look at Jud. "Two things," Guy says. "We have to try to turn the propane tank off from the outside, and radio for help."

"In that order?" Jud studies Neal.

"The tank will take two of us ... one to stand guard." There is a waver in Guy's voice, a sign that he's not entirely sure himself.

Jud is not about to reassure him. "What if we have to shoot a bear? Won't that ignite the propane?"

"Don't know. Outside, maybe not." Guy finds some resolve. "But I don't want to be sitting on a bomb in the middle of fucking nowhere. Who knows how long it'll take for the propane to bleed off and then find its way out of the Tundra Buggy."

"You're sure there's an outside shut-off valve?" Jud asks. Guy hears it again—not fear, not caution—but a note of anticipation in Jud's voice. Guy realizes that he knows next to nothing about Jud, hired by the department out of grad school at UBC. Normally Guy would find his own assistant, but someone up the ladder at Renewable Resources had recommended Jud and it was a done deal. All Guy got was a memo after the fact.

"Yeah. Let's just hope it's not frozen open ... this goddamned weather."

Guy takes the shotgun, a Winchester 870 open bore, from the closet and slides in kill loads, instead of the plastic slugs they normally use to deter bears. "Man o' man, man o' man," he repeats under his breath. These words are his worry beads. Is he doing the right thing? Maybe they should just get up the tower and radio for help? In the middle of the night and a storm on the way? "Man o' man, man o' man." To Jud he says, "Let's make this quick."

Jud adjusts his headlamp over his toque and steps onto the wooden chair under the hatch. Reaching up, he pulls himself through onto the trailer roof.

Guy hands the shotgun up to Jud. As he turns on his headlamp, he asks Allsun, "You alright?"

"Wanna puke." Her dark eyes stare out from a face the color of old snow.

"Watch out for Neal, okay ... Allsun, okay?"

"Yeah, okay ... I'm okay."

He's through the hole. The lid crashes down, silencing a wind that Allsun had taken for granted, along with the fog in her head. She's curled in a fetal sit, unsure of her muscles. Weak and sick, she fixes on the wooden chair, conjuring Guy into it. "Watch," he says. She waits for him to perform a trick.

AND HE DOES. He bashes the propane shut-off valve with a wrench, hard enough to break it off. As predicted, it was frozen open, not surprising with the thermometer deep-sixed at minus forty degrees Fahrenheit—buried in a perfectly round ocean of mercury. Guy's reasoning: better to release the propane outside into the frigid air. What he hadn't foreseen was the gas penetrating his padded, leather work mitt and leaving a painful white patch of freezer burn on his palm.

The other unknown was the polar bears. Would the sound of gas hissing from the tank attract them? Polar bears are curious. Hunters and scavengers of remarkable resource, they are eternally curious about things human. It has led them to acquire a taste for engine oil, antifreeze and vinyl seat covers, at least at this research site. The garbage dump at the town of Churchill holds other delights and dangers.

Here at Cape Churchill, the polar bears are put off their cravings by rubber bullets, plastic slugs, flares and screamers. At the dump, fire is meant to keep them away, but a starving bear is rarely put off by the smell of singed hair. These are tough beggars, requiring tough measures —high-powered rifles in less enlightened times, high-powered tranquilizer guns and polar bear jail in the age of eco-tourism.

Guy's Winchester loaded with lead slugs and large buckshot called SSG's could mean a dead bear. A dead bear at a research site dedicated to testing methods of bear deterrence that do not harm or kill would be bad luck all around. Dead bears skew stats and make for bad PR, especially when it's Nanuk of the North. It doesn't pay to mess with mystique.

The hissing from the tank has brought the bears, but not before Guy and Jud have swung up the tower ladder to the plywood platform twelve feet above the ground. Here, they are barely out of range of a hind-leg-standing, one thousand-pound male with a Muhammed-Ali reach that does more than sting like a bee. With paws the size of catcher mitts and claws the color and cutting cleverness of the black volcanic glass, obsidian, the polar bear is not a worthy opponent, it's a worthy predator.

From the plywood platform, nicknamed "the launching pad," the men watch in awe as snowdrifts out on the tundra shift, stand and trot toward camp. Curled up, the wind whipping their exposed backs, the bears have still heard or smelled or sensed change.

Carried on the wind is the smell of snow. Guy turns to the north and the approaching blizzard, out of sight behind a phalanx of dark sky. He feels betrayed, as if nature is conspiring against him. A howl of despair rises in his throat. He quickly swallows it. Guy senses that if he were to give in to his rage, his assistant would somehow find it gratifying. Jud seems tightly strung, someone who would see self-control as a sign of power.

ALLSUN IS ASLEEP beside Neal, her fingers, no longer gloved, resting on his lips. Blood crusted, against bloodless lips, her fingers resemble flames meant to flicker in his breath. If rescuers came, ripping off the plywood that seals the trailer door against bears (nailed in place after Jane), unaware of the hatch secreted in the roof; if they broke the seal of rubber weather-stripping, swung back the door to the ATCO tomb, would they find an arctic

Romeo and Juliet? No. Neal and Allsun are friends; brought together and held in thrall, literally, by Allsun's husband, Damon. Damon the Greek god, Damon the monstrously beautiful vegetable.

The first time Allsun saw Damon, he was naked. He stood in the middle of the room surrounded by studious eyes. She was late, the studio crowded, so she remained at the door and watched. What else could she do? She couldn't take her eyes off him.

Her drawing instructor had caught sight of her. Beckoning her forward, he placed Allsun and her drawing board at Damon's feet. It seemed there was no other space, other than the doorway, which Allsun felt would have done fine. Especially when she noted a snigger here and there from behind easels and drawing pads. Had her instructor done this on purpose, placed her maddeningly close because he recognized the look on her face? Was she meant to look foolish? Well, why should she? This was art! This was awesome!

Hers was a unique perspective, looking up the planes of his body to a face she had to tilt her head back to see. She decided to be true to the perspective. His kneecaps at eye level were huge compared to the tapering down to his feet and the tapering away to the small point that was his head. Allsun chuckled at this thought. And when she glanced up to marry the lines of his face with her pencil, he was watching her. Had he heard her?

The Greek god stepped down from his pedestal, a small platform, really. His hour was up. She watched him make a hasty retreat toward a pile of clothes on a chair. Had he heard her?

Dressed and ready to leave, he stopped by where she

remained on the floor, finishing a series of cartoons of him dressing. "I see," was his response to her sketches.

Allsun didn't look up. "What do you see?"

"What you were laughing at." He stood over her.

"Oh?"

"Those freckles," he pointed to the inside of his right thigh, "look like an acrobat . . . maybe a clown."

Slowly she raised her head to take him in. "You mean those crumbs from my eraser?"

He knelt down, putting his face close to examine the page. He flicked the freckles with a fingernail. "Now they look like two people having coffee."

He was so close Allsun was navigating the Minotaur's maze of his right ear with her eyes. "When?"

"An hour. In the Jungle." He was up and moving away. "I'm late for a tutorial."

He was gone, nameless, despite the intimate images in her hands. Wasn't that just like art—to leave concrete proof of a mystery?

Jud

JUD POPS DOWN the roof hatch like a stoat down a hole. He's brought up short, still standing on the chair. Lying there on the floor, Allsun and Neal could be dead. Jud reviews what this would mean, then breaks the spell by jumping down and passing his bare hand over each face. There is breath. He checks pulses. Allsun's is stronger than Neal's is. He sits on the chair, takes up the vigil.

ALL THROUGH THAT first year back with his father, Jud would wake in the middle of the night, walk casually, as if going down the hall to the bathroom for a glass of water, into his father's bedroom. He would let his hand rest inches above his father's face like a mirror meant to capture the exhalation of life.

Knowing his father breathed, he would sit in the dark room contemplating the man's death. It was an old habit, developed first in his grandfather's house and then in the boarding schools that had been part of the adult bargain struck over him. He reasoned that if his father were dead, if he were orphaned, he could live with his grandparents instead of being a boarder and a visitor.

Through all those dorm nights he honed the ways and means of killing his father. The school library was crammed with history books that described machines of destruction, atrocities, torture, death in every shape. These books fed the black films of his nights with the "ways," but the "means" came from J.G. Frazer's *The Golden Bough*. Frazer brought it all together for Jud's locked-away mind. He stole *The Golden Bough* from the library and kept it hidden in the false bottom of his private trunk. The book was his manual. The secret compartment was courtesy of his grandfather, who understood the necessity of a private place when one was forced into anonymity. Grandfather Harmon had served in the Korean War.

The time had come, or so he thought, at seventeen, when he rejoined his father. In that first year, he reread and read again *The Golden Bough*, preparing to follow the prescription of the Aborigines of Southeastern Australia who believed that "a man may be injured by burying sharp fragments of quartz, glass, and so forth in the marks made by his reclining body." It would be easy. His father never made his bed in the mornings.

The other thing that kept him sitting in a chair in his father's 3:00 a.m. room was the thought of his father's work, the "cause" that he, the child Jud, had been sacrificed to, just like Isaac on the notion of God. In coming back—he could never say *home* to Vancouver—Jud had come to know his father's work outside the context of his grandparents' disparaging cant. Jud was interested. He realized that it wasn't time yet.

Guy

FINALLY GUY REACHES a nurse on the night desk at the Churchill Health Centre's hospital. She leaves him hanging on the thin line of fear while she looks for the intern.

The voice of a young doctor comes crackling across the tundra. "'Remove victim from exposure. Administer artificial respiration if breathing has stopped. Keep at rest . . .' Get them the hell in here!"

"No land vehicle out here. We'll have to get a chopper."

"Not likely till this storm blows through."

"I know. So what do I do?"

"Just what you've been doing. Monitor respiration and heartbeat." The doctor pauses.

"Yes?"

"Hold on . . . 'Inhalation exposure to propane in high concentrations may cause central nervous system disorder, for example, loss of coordination, weakness, fatigue, mental confusion, blurred vision and cardiac arrhythmias. May cause irritation, breathing failure, coma and death.' Monitor around the clock . . . be prepared to perform AR again. That's as much as I can tell you."

"Shit."

"We're talking by radio, right? Keep me posted if you can . . . Dr. Thomas . . ."

"Yeah, thanks." Guy breaks the connection. He checks his watch: 4 a.m. Two hours before he can reach Conrad Cain at the Churchill airstrip.

At a loss, he paces. Then he remembers Neal calling Allsun *Jane*. God, Neal still dreams about her. A short laugh, almost a bark, echoes off the plywood walls, reminding him he's alone in the tower hut. But never alone, especially out on this lonely spit of land. Neal calls out for Jane; well, he'll find her in Guy's nightmares.

That might surprise Neal. They haven't talked much over the last few years, gone their separate ways after university—Guy into government, Northwest Territories Renewable Resources, Neal into the gas and oil industry. Separated by the twenty degrees of latitude between Calgary and Inuvik, but reunited here at the Cape through the profession they share. Haunted by the same ghost. Somewhere in between is what's left of a friendship. On which of the invisible lines of latitude would he place it—at halfway or one of the diminishing markers?

Guy has never been comfortable in small rooms. They force his sensibilities inward. One hundred square feet is not enough space in which to think straight—the lab trailer will be worse. Damnable weather. He should be outside burning rancid seal meat on the makeshift barbecue to entice the bears in from the edge of Hudson Bay to be counted, marked, studied and deterred. A lost day could jeopardize this year's research program. And then there is the mixed blessing of the media, who will eat up more of his precious time. A vicious circle—media interest could give the Bear Safety Program the kind of profile that attracts funding, but his work here could suffer. This kind of storm meant that within days the bears would move on, abandoning land for ice.

With the change in weather, the inland sea that stretches to the horizon will join the land in a show of solidarity—a frozen plain of water polar bears inhabit gladly, for now they can hunt seals, now they can eat after nearly eight months of starvation. At freeze-up the bears walk on water, way out and away from this tit of land. Protruding into the Bay, the Cape attracts new ice that forms in the north and is shunted south by strong winds. The polar bears know this. Normally solitary animals, they congregate at the Cape in October, restlessly awaiting the ice.

Guy strips the sleeping bags from the bunks in the tower hut, rolls them both together and ties them with one of the drawstrings. He stuffs them into a backpack. He's going to need both hands on the tower ladder. The wind is blowing so hard that the tower sways like a conductor, the steel guy wires screaming a storm symphony worthy of the Valkyries.

He pulls his hood up as he steps onto the landing; the hut door flies out of his hand, smashing inward against the counter, tinned goods rolling onto the floor. Guy curses the door shut and faces wind-driven snow. He could swear it's not snow pitting his skin but sand from the spit.

Normally, he would swing down the ladder like a tailless gibbon. From his early years negotiating the rungs of his dad's grain silos, he is accustomed to scant stairways. But the wind keeps him off balance and the snow ices the rungs. When he thinks of the flatland farm boy transplanted to the Rocky Mountains, there is a hint of a smile. A sentinel among sentinels, his watch took him up the ladders of fire lookouts all the summers of his first university degree.

On the plywood platform he must fight the storm, pushing his body through the onslaught to reach the trailer roof and the hatch. It reminds him of the human convulsion of a Calcutta street at rush hour—a black hole of suffocation.

He struggles against rising panic at the memory. It makes him clumsy in removing the backpack and opening the hatch. The light slaps him out of the darkness. He slides down the hole after the pack with more urgency than he cares to show his waiting assistant.

Jud has fallen asleep, and the plummeting backpack hits him like a load of bricks, not feathers. Jolted out of his desertion of duty, he does a rapid check on Neal and Allsun as Guy descends out of the maelstrom.

To Jud, Guy appears particularly grim; perhaps it's just that he's set his jaw against their ill luck, or Mother Nature, or both. Jud knows this might be the end of the eleventh annual polar bear study at Cape Churchill. What is more dire, what would have Guy gnashing his teeth, is a setback to the bear detection and deterrence research. This is a funding renewal year for the internationally successful program that Guy manages, but the federal government's Department of Environment is under review and all funding is frozen. Jud grins to himself at the appropriateness of the word *frozen*. Frozen in poisoned sleep on the floor of the lab trailer is Guy's other hope. Neal, as chairman of the committee on Bear Conflict Management, is in a position to recommend the

Bear Safety Program to oil and gas companies with interests in the high Arctic and with research dollars to spend.

Guy kneels. He has yet to push the hood of his parka off his face. Looking down the fur-lined tunnel at Neal and Allsun, for a moment he feels removed, a safe distance from their distress and his amenability. A whisper, "Oh, God," is as close as he gets to a prayer.

Guy throws back his hood. "Any change?" he asks Jud.

"No." Jud looks at the backpack. "Not really." He is hoping for a thermos of tea.

His disappointment is not visible when Guy straightens up and empties the backpack. Jud learned inscrutability early in life.

Guy covers Neal and Allsun, folding the backpack into a pillow that he fusses under Allsun's head as she sleeps—altogether too soundly for Guy, who still has the word *coma* crackling in his ear—on her side, one arm thrown over Neal, not careless in attitude, but somehow intimate, perhaps protective. "Nothing more we can do," he mutters.

"Pardon?" Jud sharpens his gaze on Guy.

"Wait . . . all we can do is wait."

"You talked to somebody?"

"Yeah . . . watch and wait . . . check their vital signs. And AR . . . you know how to give mouth to mouth, don't you?"

"Yeah. I'm certified."

"Good. I'll go back up the tower in a couple of hours and make breakfast." Guy surveys the trailer. "We have to adjust our schedule. See what can be done while the weather's bad." He realizes he needs to talk about the work. Being in the lab trailer with bear bone, blood and tooth, these bits of stolen detritus draw him like amulets back into the world of the great white bear.

There is magic in this land, a magic that he cannot convey to the likes of funding officers, boards, committees. More the pity. If truth be told, he is probably more concerned about what will happen to the bears in human-bear conflicts. We humans are pernicious. We have become a rogue animal compared to the polar bear, which fits into this place with a perfection that would make Buddha cry. If Guy were of another time and place, he would have been an arctic shaman capable of rising above humanness to walk with the bear. Instead he is a man of science who feels the pressure of a world changing faster than he can come to know it. He's working against a clock set in motion by pollution. Rising levels of toxic chemicals in the oceans threaten many species, including the polar bear, whose diet is almost exclusively seals. Climate changes are creating shorter arctic winters, giving the bears less time on the ice to hunt. Guy is aware of a declining birth rate among polar bears and a drop in the average body weight.

Guy fingers a tooth pried from the jaw of a drugged female bear during a routine survey of the Owl River maternity denning site. He rubs the rough edges where Jud has sawed away a slice for analysis. Under the microscope, he can read the history of bear N61 the way an arborist reads a tree. A sliver of calcium reveals just how long this female has been adapting to snow and ice, feast and famine, hibernation and motherhood. Pegged by her tooth rings, she has seen six summers of midnight suns. Twice the number of arctic winters he's dreamed

through. As he replaces the tooth, Guy says to Jud, "Let's finish compiling and documenting the data we have. Look for gaps. When the weather breaks we can fill them."

"So we're scrapping our scheduled program?"

"The storm's setting the timetable now. Gotta be adaptable out here." Guy squeezes passed Jud sitting on the wooden chair under the hatch. He rubs his hands together while blowing on his fingertips. His breath stings the white spot of propane freezer-burn on one palm. Kneeling, he places his fingers on Neal's neck and counts the beats off against the second hand of his watch. He repeats this check with Allsun. Both pulses are still erratic.

Guy turns back to Jud. "I'll start reviewing the data while you finish up the lab work." He picks up a binder and pulls a stool out from under the counter.

Jud would rather take a power nap. He hasn't slept in twenty-four hours. Too much excitement. Too much to do. He pulls the parsimonious wooden chair over to the make-do plywood counter, arranging it in front of the microscope, a dated, no-frills piece of scientific equipment that is symbolic of this whole research project as far as he can see.

Busying himself preparing samples for the microscope, Jud wonders how he got here. He sniggers. Guy's head comes up from the data binder he's reading. Jud notices from the corner of his eye that Guy is watching him, and covers by clearing his throat.

His childhood had been *some* preparation. When his father sold him to his American grandparents for twenty thousand dollars, Trevor Ash didn't lie, didn't tell his ten-year-old son it was for his own good now that his mother was dead. The word that left its mark like a fingerprint in Plasticine was *sacrifice*, as in "We all have to make sacrifices ... your mother did ... and now I must. You are my Isaac." Jud had come to learn later who his father's god was.

Weighed up on the altar of his father's ideals, Jud was a small part of what it took to ransom the earth. It was the late 'sixties; his parents were in the forefront of the Vancouver peace movement. His father wrote for an underground newspaper, his mother practiced civil disobedience with the young Jud in tow. In his eco-warrior column in the *Georgia Strait*, Trevor Ash made it clear that only bold acts would free the earth from the rapacious grasp of big business and its sycophant, government.

In 1970, his father was conspiring with others of like mind to form an organization, a protest organization that needed money and a boat to do battle with the American government over nuclear testing in the Aleutians.

And so Jud was shipped out. Put on a ferry to Seattle, his father's parting gift in his lap—a second-hand copy of *Warriors of the Rainbow: Strange and Prophetic Dreams of the Indian Peoples*. Between the pages of the book was a sealed envelope addressed to Judge Cleveland Harmon, Jud's maternal grandfather.

Jud opened the letter, his own act of disobedience, and read the terms of his sale. He was not to live with his grandparents, under their "direct and unrelenting brainwashing," but was to be sent to a boarding school that offered a first-rate liberal education. There were other provisos concerning holidays, visits and the like, that led to the final paragraph in this letter of demands: "... under no circumstances are you to change my son's name. Consider the memory of your daughter. Do not even think of altering what she cherished. With love she named our child. I'll not let you take this from her. William Blake was a visionary. Our son will live up to his name."

The first thing Judge Cleveland Harmon did was file papers for legal custody of his grandson and apply to the courts to have the boy's name changed. Blake Ash became Judson Harmon Ash, named for the U.S. Attorney General of 1895, Judson Harmon—a name he could truly live up to.

Judson Blake Harmon Ash called himself Isaac, but never out loud, except when he re-enacted Jehovah's test of Abraham. The forest surrounding Harmon House, outside of Seattle, was made for secrets. The rain forest of the Pacific West Coast—British Columbia, Washington, Oregon—is a temperate jungle. There, the secretive child with many names made a world of his own. He built an altar of stones. He offered up small animals that replaced him in the sight of God. His sacrifices of blood and fire kept him safe, and as he grew older they made him invincible. In his domain he grew confident, self-sufficient and ruthless. He still has a need for animal blood on his hands.

GUY'S MIND WANDERS. He reads and rereads sentences, whole paragraphs. Columns of figures could be animal tracks in snow. His eyes fall on Neal and Allsun, and for a moment he feels like a voyeur. They look like lovers asleep together, a thought that evokes an image of

Damon. Immediately he directs his attention back to his work: Damon is more pain than he can deal with here and now.

Guy speaks to wall off his thoughts behind the brick and mortar of words. "I don't know how she made it up that ladder."

Jud remains an extension of metal and mirrors, not moving his eye from the microscope. "What? Allsun?"

"Yeah, by all rights she should never have made it across the gangplank . . . dizzy . . . disoriented. Climbing experience . . . instinct . . . body knowledge."

Jud looks away from his task. "Body knowledge? What's that?"

On one level, Guy had been talking to himself. He considers Jud. "Physical prowess so ingrained, so habitual, you can take it for granted."

"She's a mountain climber?" Jud returns to the microcosm to which he has reduced bear N61.

Guy hears *she*, not Allsun, but the stripped down *she*, as impersonal as a piece of tissue locked between glass slides. He studies his assistant, who is bent over the workbench: tall, lean, strong; just how strong Guy recognized the day Jud flew in with the supplies and together they had unloaded the Twin Otter. The face belies the body: a moon face stark in its roundness, because Jud has shaved his head, except for a forelock of white-blond curls. Finally Guy says, "Ice. Allsun likes hardwater. Good too, the ice scares her shitless, keeps her honest. She's got the pictures to prove it." Guy is not sure why he adds this last provision, tinged with a shade of challenge.

"Yeah." Jud is off-hand, seemingly preoccupied.

Guy feels the need to say more and hates the impulse,

"Won an award at the Mountain Film Festival for a series of black and white stills of a climb on Polar Circus."

"Funny name."

"What? Oh, yeah, I guess . . . serious shit, though . . . vertical ice, avalanches."

THEY HAD EMBRACED the New Year struggling to ascend Polar Circus. Allsun had put the idea forward mostly because she wanted to shoot this spectacular frozen waterfall. But she sold it to the rest of them as a symbol of the arduous upward climb on the slippery slope of their doctoral degrees. They didn't need a hard sell. Hell, they were primed for adventure. Close to the end of long years of study and research, they were more than ready to break out. New Year's Day 1982, prophetic in a strange way.

Guy led, Damon climbed second on the rope, Neal belayed from the ground, and Allsun photographed. She called them the three bears, and it fit, although they would have preferred Dumas's legend of *The Three Musketeers* to a fairy tale.

All bear biologists, Guy was easily Papa Bear, Neal the mediator could be considered Mama Bear, and Damon, younger than the other two and more high-spirited, certainly was Baby Bear. That made Allsun Goldilocks, the men countered. But she didn't fit the description: she wasn't a blonde but a redhead, and never had she been gormless, nor was she afraid of bears, at least these three bears. They conceded on all counts except on the charge of gormlessness—how could they know—she was a recent addition to their fairy tale.

But when they thought about it, they had to agree they couldn't imagine Allsun lacking in sense, in that girlie, Grimm, Goldilocks fashion. Five-foot-ten in stature, they doubted there had been a time when she skipped through the woods. Allsun would have lined this folksy, cutesy image up in the sights of her rifle as if it were a paper target and shot it through the heart, then risen from the hard-packed snow, slung her rifle over her shoulder and skated her skis onto the track. Allsun had been a biathlete, and what's more, a Canadian Junior biathlon champion. The men teased her, calling her "bi." Well, except for Damon.

Her physicality, her intensity, balanced Damon's classical good looks and witty sense of humor. Guy and Neal envied their friend, but shared his joy when Baby Bear married Goldilocks that summer.

From below, Allsun shot the climbers as if they were occlusions in a glass sculpture of gigantic proportions. She was preparing to put away her camera and take over belaying the rope from Neal when she heard it. Guy's ice axe, instead of making the solid *thunk* of a curved and serrated blade in ice, made only a *ping* when he swung it into the hardwater above his head. The wrong sound. Fragile ice. A dinnerplate sheared off and Frisbeed down onto Damon below. The circle of ice hit his helmet hard, throwing his head back. His upper body fell away from the iceface, suspending him by the wrist loops attached to his ice axes, both embedded in the waterfall just seconds before.

Allsun lunged for the rope. She clipped the locking carabiner on the front of her harness into a loop she tied off in the played-out rope. Grabbed her ice axes, which were planted in a snow bank, and started up, preempting the safety signals she should have exchanged with Neal of "On Belay," "Climbing," "Climb On."

By the time she reached Damon, he was shaking his head and groping for the handles of his ice axes.

"Jesus, they held," Damon said. Allsun was cranking an ice screw into the icefall beside him. She clipped the rope into the knob of the ice screw, giving her and Damon added protection.

"You alright?" Allsun monkey hung on her ice axes and the steel front-points of her crampons.

"Yeah . . . I . . . yeah, I think so. Didn't see it coming. Hold on." Damon pulled his right foot out of the ice and kicked it back in, reestablishing the crampon front-point in the plastic ice.

"Saw stars," he said. "Highway to the stars."

They both laughed.

"Guess you're climbing third?"

"Guess I am." Allsun willed the tremor out of her voice.

"Cover my ass?" He gave her a smile that took her all the way back to the Jungle and their first coffee.

"With pleasure."

They had chosen to climb from the valley floor instead of cheating by walking up a ramp of rock and snow to the left of the gully and thereby avoiding the mostly 70-degree ice that formed the bottom section of the waterfall. When they reached the snow basin that curved up to the second chunk of Polar Circus, a 150-foot icefall, they took a quick break for food and water.

Allsun was relieved to see Damon eating and drinking, a sign that he'd shaken off the effects of head-butting a piece of crystal.

The route dictated that they complete section two before nightfall and bivouac at the second snow basin in two caves, one of ice, one of rock.

The little band of axe-wielding friends made it with just enough light left to get the Primus stoves going, boil up some freeze-dried food and sigh into their sleeping bags with a cup of tea. Huddled behind a beard of ice hanging from the underside of a jutting rock chin, they talked about their work, about lining up job interviews —a bittersweet topic.

"Hey, Allsun Skelly Pythias, what happens if Damon lands a job in the Arctic? You going to settle down, keep your man warm and give the Pythias clan the babies they expect?" Neal smirked behind his cup of tea.

Allsun studied the shadow and light, the full moon a spot light on a glass curtain. She had not found a focus for her artistic sensibilities yet. In casting about, she hadn't considered the Arctic, not until lately.

"Well," she said finally, hearing their unease in the shifting of nylon on snow, "Damon would be a long, long way from Mama Sophronia. And the rest of the Pythias clan."

The three bears chuffed in laughter.

"*Touché, ma petite shoe.*" Damon slugged her on the arm, his fist enclosed in a down mitt that looked like a boxing glove. He continued his animated voice imitation of his favorite cartoon character, Pepe Le Pew, "Ah, *ma chérie*, I will take you away from all this. We will find heaven together."

"Whoa, watch you don't melt the ice." Guy was up, sliding his sleeping bag into a protective bivy sac, a fitted tent without poles. He was preparing to take his gear up into the rock cave where he and Neal would sleep. The ledge behind the bridal veil of ice was only big enough for two to stretch out.

Settled in with Allsun, Damon spoke from the depths of his sleeping bag. "Where do you want to be, Al?"

"Hmm." Allsun had been drifting. "Together ... then we'll see."

"You know, Guy's going for that job with Renewable Resources."

"Wondered why he got all busy when Neal made that crack about the Arctic. So, you going to compete against him?"

"Don't know. I thought you might have made that decision for me."

"Really?" Allsun was suddenly alert.

"No, well, not entirely. But it's hard. The three of us ... trying to start careers all at the same time."

"What about Neal?"

"Doesn't want to go north." Damon's words hung in the crystalline air between them.

"Because of Jane?"

"Maybe. He hasn't said."

"No, and he won't." Allsun's breath hooked white lace around the top edge of her sleeping bag.

"Haven't heard him say her name once since the accident."

"God, what a year it's been. This next one will be better." Sleep pulled her toward happier times.

"I'll drink to that," Damon's voice was lost down the rabbit hole of his sleeping bag.

"When we get down off this mountain."

"Back where it's safe and ..."

A.

ALLSUN HAD BEEN photographing the mountains across the valley as alpenglow turned ice and snow to fire, when she suddenly realized Damon had not stirred. Normally the first one up, it was unlike him to miss a red-glorious sunrise.

"Get out here, Day-Glo," she called. "Come see ..."

Damon groaned. A thrill went through Allsun, a dart of apprehension. She listened, then took the camera from her eye and disappeared behind the veil of ice. He was still in his sleeping bag.

"Damon? Damon, you okay?"

His head slowly became visible. The light made him moan. "Got a stinking headache."

"Maybe you slept funny? You know, your neck ..."

Allsun jumped back as Damon suddenly sat up and vomited.

"My god, Day, what's wrong?" She fished a roll of toilet paper from her pack and began cleaning up his sleeping bag before the spew could freeze in place.

"Don't know." Damon looked as if he wanted to make a joke but couldn't marshal the words. As Allsun wiped him like a nylon-swaddled baby, he finally said, "Bad freeze-dried."

She stopped to look at him. "Do you think?"

He groaned, "No, not possible."

"Then what?"

"Guy's dinnerplate."

"You said you were fine." Allsun examined his face.

"I was. Had a headache, but nothing like this." Damon smiled thinly.

"We have to get you down."

"No. Make some tea. I'll get up and shake it off."

"Damon, it's not smart to stay." She remained steadfastly in his line of vision.

"Just give me some time, okay?" He was impatient now. Then he touched her arm gently. "We'll see," Damon said.

By the time Guy and Neal arrived behind the glowing screen of ice, Damon professed he felt better. Allsun didn't believe him.

As they roped up to walk the narrow snow gully to The Pencil, she watched him fumble as he adjusted his harness and clipped the biner through the rope. She swallowed repeatedly, but the lump lodged in her gullet just above her heart would not slip down.

Allsun made them stop so she could photograph The Pencil, an icicle worthy of the most cold-blooded writer. It hung free for 150 feet from a rock fist. Six feet in diameter, it was suspended above jottings of ice, a massive accumulation called The Pedestal in the guidebook.

Allsun purposely took her time in order to give Damon a rest and to keep him off the icefall long enough for her to be sure about his condition.

This was her ploy: photographing everything in sight, slowing their progress past The Pencil and up the 100-foot pitch on the right side of The Pedestal with its short vertical section.

Once they reached the steep snow bowls, she put her camera away. This was no place to go slowly. These bowls were avalanche prone, and the team crossed them swiftly. Not a word was uttered, none of the normal banter and curses echoed up the incised ravines.

They were set to traverse some 200 feet right and up to a shadow of small trees. Bringing up the rear, Allsun watched Damon stumble along, his enduring grace, his sure-footedness gone. They would make the trees and she would enlist the others to convince him to abandon the climb.

The cluster of spartan spruce provided some protection. The friends stopped and huddled together so she could photograph them. She knew this would be their summit shot. Through the camera, she could see Damon's eyes—a blinking, idiot stare.

Allsun returned to the group, put her camera away and turned to Guy. "We're going back down."

"What?"

"Look at Damon's eyes. He's had a blinding headache since yesterday. Now he's clumsy, stumbling, barely on his feet."

Guy peered into Damon's face. "Shit. You stupid bugger, why didn't you say?"

Allsun answered, "It didn't get bad till this morning." Damon wasn't to be blamed.

"It's okay," Neal stepped in, calmly voicing the next step. "We're in good shape here. We got the trees ... we can set up a rappel."

"And the guide book says there's bolts in the gully," Allsun added, relieved they were turning back.

"If we can find them." Guy knelt beside Damon. "Hey, old bud, got some jam? We're going to do a bit of rappelling."

Ropes slung around trees and off various climbing bolts hammered into solid rock by climbers on the first few ascents, held them as they backed down the mountain. Damon managed to keep his legs between him and the rock and ice as they descended.

At the bottom of the mountain face, their relief was short-lived. It started to snow.

In some ways, the ski down the creek bed to the Jeep Commando parked across from the Cirrus Mountain cook shelter was more of an ordeal than the rappelled descent had been. Damon fell repeatedly as his coordination diminished. Snow, bullied by the wind, rushed up the creek-carved gap in the trees. Visibility was the length of a ski.

The highway was no better. Guy drove as fast as the black ice and blowing snow on the snaking Banff-Jasper Highway would allow. Allsun sat in the back seat with Damon, forcing him to stay awake.

Out of the absolute dark of moonless mountain valleys, they arrived into the misplaced light of Banff and its hospital.

JUD SENSES THE stillness. For a moment, he's dappled in comfort—sun diffused by giant leaves and ancient cedars. Memory becomes a shiver up his spine. He turns to look at Guy as if he had spoken. But the other man is lost behind closed eyes.

What had they been talking about minutes ago? Mountains? Climbing . . . yes, ice climbing. Well, he looks the type—worn hiking boots, wrecked anoraks, the smell of wet wool—probably doesn't own a suit. For all that, his "boss" is not to be underestimated; he has nerve and a canniness Jud associates with the Oregon fruit farmers he worked for during summer vacations.

Average in height, but built like a brick shithouse; Jud suspects Guy is a farmboy raised on chores, on hard, physical labor. It's in his walk, as if his hips and legs are a flatbed truck meant to haul the heavy load of a well-fed, muscled trunk—a smooth economy of movement from the waist down.

Jud contemplates checking Neal's and Allsun's vital signs; instead he works over the nature of their relationship with Guy. He knows they were all at university together, but what about now? Have they come together simply because they were assigned to this project? Or are they still close?

Under Jud's scrutiny, Guy blinks as if his eyes had not closed. "What?"

"Just checking on our patients." Jud slides from the chair.

"That's okay, I'll do it." Guy pulls off his fingerless, ragg-wool gloves.

Jud decides to put his musings to the test. "You an ice climber too?" he says to Guy's back as he bends over Allsun and Neal.

"Hmm." Guy is counting beats. "Yeah."

"Not much of that up in Inuvik, I'd guess." Jud watches Guy check the circulation to Allsun's hands, chafing warmth into them.

"No." Guy reclaims his seat on the stool. He looks down at Allsun and Neal. "Last time was the three of us." Guy is not inclined to breathe life into memory with speech, but Jud is showing an interest. "Allsun got the last of the Polar Circus shots."

"You did Polar Circus?" Jud leans back in the chair, stretching his long legs to occupy the remaining floor space.

"Twice. We got halfway up the first time. Allsun's

husband, Damon, got hurt . . . we had to bring him down." There is a line, as if Guy had taken a magic marker to a calendar, drawing a halt to time. He dwells in the days before Jane's death and Damon's descent into the netherworld of PVS. Guy would prefer to recount their golden days, but unfortunately, he's introduced Jud to Polar Circus.

"Geez, tough break." Jud has registered Guy's reluctance. "So, he didn't do the second climb?"

In looking away from his heavily scarred hands and up at Jud, Guy confronts reality. "Not the second climb, no. He's comatose ...persistent vegetative state for the last four years. We finished the climb for him." Guy can see it there on the summit—Damon's tribute—his blue cotton bandanna knotted in the eye of a bolt the three of them took turns hammering into the rock. A blue scrap of cloth stained with his sweat, trailing in the wind like a prayer.

"What happened? He fall?"

Guy, confused, comes down off the summit of Polar Circus. "Fall? No ...you mean the first climb? No ...hit with a piece of falling ice ...mild concussion."

"But ..."

"Damon was attacked . . . clubbed over the head." Damon alone in the lab, working late. Damon alone at the end of the long corridor, at the end of a tunnel.

"You mean ..."

"Intruders into the Biology Department's vivarium." Guy pauses over the rising bile in his throat. "Liberated," he jeers. "The lab animals." Regaining his cool, he adds, "According to the spray paint on the wall."

Jud stares at Allsun as if seeing her for the first time. "Liberated," he repeats under his breath.

GUY IS CLIMBING the tower ladder and feeling less useless than when he sat ruminating in the lab trailer. He will radio the airport, get a weather report, a message to Conrad Cain. The storm has settled into a dull roar. It's powered up and now it's cruising. When a blizzard steadies out like this, it can go on forever or quit in a minute. No telling.

But that won't do. Guy needs a fixed point, a time to plan toward. He has lost what he values highly in himself—patience. And he can't understand why. He has been in tight spots before, some of them with Allsun and Neal, and he kept it together. This time feels different; he senses . . . what? Trouble? Disaster? Even the wind sandpapering his face seems wrong somehow: "An ill wind blows no good."

"Hell, Mom, not now," he says to the wind. But her voice comes unbidden into his mind again: "Darker than the inside of a black cow at midnight"; "It's a tree-snappin' night"; "It's a cold wind to calf your ass against"; "That wind's strong enough to blow the nuts off a gang plow." His mother's homilies get Guy as far as the tower hut door, where he stands and laughs against the wind. She had that effect on him. One of the funniest pessimists he has ever known.

In the tower hut, he goes about the business of radioing the airport. His spirit is resurrected by a friendly human voice reassuring him that the storm is a blowhard . . . bluster and back off.

Guy talks to himself as he mixes up powdered eggs and opens a can of baked beans. "Get Al and Neal to the hospital, get the project back on track, it'll all work out." Then he remembers the media, looks at his watch for the date. "Man o' man, Chuck Ford is due today, his film crew tomorrow, Suzuki the day after. Hell's bells. He should never have agreed to this media circus. Yeah, and money grows on trees, Guy. Damn politicians . . . can't manage their way out of a wet paper bag. No more grant money until the Auditor General has done his number on Environment and its dumb-ass minister." He decides on something stronger than tea. Retrieving his stash of real coffee, he opens the can and spoons liberal grounds into a paper filter. "Give me strength" is his incantation as he pours boiling water from the kettle into the plastic cone holding the filter.

Guy drinks coffee while he prepares a breakfast of scrambled eggs and warmed-over baked beans on the two-burner Coleman stove. Never mind a pan for the beans; he strips off the paper label and puts the tin can directly on the burner over the propane flame.

BACK IN THE lab trailer, Guy unloads his backpack, pulling out a plastic container of eggs and beans, a Mason jar of coffee, a plate, a cup, a fork. When he unscrews the lid from the jar, Jud turns abruptly from the microscope. "Coffee?" he asks tentatively, as if the fragrance is a figment of his imagination.

"Yeah, put hair on your chest," Guy jokes. "Figured we deserved something stronger than tea." He takes charge. "After the night we've had."

"Ah-huh." Jud accepts the cup of coffee from Guy.

"I'm going back up the tower to wait for a call from Conrad. As soon as it comes in, I'll spell you off down here and you can go sack out." Guy checks Allsun and

Neal. No change. He was hoping their erratic heartbeats would have become at least regular, if not normal. Not knowing what to expect erodes his optimism, cutting frown lines between his eyebrows.

JUD DRINKS THE first cup of coffee greedily. The buzz he gets reminds him that his stomach is empty. He pops the lid off the plastic container, lifts the fork. Sprawled in the chair, he contemplates Allsun while he forks and chews, forks and chews, ignoring the taste of the food. PVS, he thinks, four years, a vegetable. Time does not stand still, there is only gain or loss. Jud had gained on that night in February and it appeared the man he struck had lost.

THE RAID ON the University of Calgary had been Jud's true initiation. His unit had cleaned the vivarium out. When he got back to Oregon, he was no longer a recruit, but a full-fledged LIB soldier. On reporting that he had struck a man with a tire iron during the encounter, he was reminded that casualities were a fact of war. During the operation, he had cursed the man's presence; it had fouled his meticulous plan.

Reconnaissance had been dead easy. Jud had graduated the spring before from the University of British Columbia and was familiar with the workings of a university Biology Department. He simply pretended to be a student at the University of Calgary. There was next to no security, so he would wander the halls or sit on the floor, his back against a locker, appearing to consume *Readings in Wildlife Conservation*.

He would often make his way to the solarium, a humid, tropical jungle at the heart of the administration building. He liked to sit among students and professors as they drank coffee and bounced words off the glass ceiling and each other, while he drew maps and made detailed notes. He knew what they didn't. He would do what they would not. It gave him a sense of power not unlike the feeling he had experienced as a child, sacrificing animals in his grandfather's woodlot.

Armed with a tire iron to break the one flimsy lock on the vivarium door, Jud had led four other eco-soldiers through the maze of halls. The animals were housed at the end of a corridor beyond six laboratories, three on each side. Before running the gauntlet, Jud stopped the unit so he could listen. All he heard was their quarry—caged monkeys teasing caged dogs into fits of barking, which in turn agitated caged cats, rabbits, rats, mice. This is exactly what he expected at two in the morning.

They had approached the vivarium quickly, their sneakers skidding on the polished linoleum floor. Midway down the corridor, a man in a white lab coat stepped out a laboratory door. Surprised into action, Jud had swung the tire iron without uttering a word.

Two more years with LIB had given Jud the kind of training and network his father had hoped for. Having moved up the ranks, Jud was sent back to Canada with orders to recruit and train the first Canadian unit of LIB. His cover: graduate student in wildlife conservation.

JUD LIKES HIS double life, smiles at the now familiar thrill of having the upper hand. Thanks to Guy, Jud now knows about Allsun and her partner, the man ... Damon, the man he clubbed in the vivarium raid; she doesn't know about him. No one does who doesn't deserve to. He's taken great pains to keep his association with LIB a secret. "A secret society" is what his father calls it, visualizing the monks of war, the Knights Templar. He humors his father; there is no place for the cross in Jud's vision. He has fallen like fruit from *The Golden Bough*; the priest king is his icon, not the Red Friars.

Nevertheless, Jud listens when his father quotes from the books he reads. There is always something to be learned. Two pieces of history according to Desmond Seward's *The Monks of War* have stayed with him: "The Templars found themselves heroes almost overnight. Europe was thrilled by these holy warriors who guarded the throne of David. Death in battle was martyrdom, a road traveled by 20,000 Templars in two centuries." And, "They neglected to live, but were prepared to die in the service of Christ." Make a man a hero and he will give you his life. The price of this lesson went way beyond a mere 20,000 men.

ALLSUN MOANS AND flings her arm out.

Jud jumps out of the way. "Shit," he says. He exhales a nervous laugh and examines Allsun's face, searching for signs of incrimination. Perhaps, in her sleep state, she had been picking up on his thoughts. He'd have to be more careful. "Thoughts are things," he reminds himself. Jud takes a deep breath, closes his eyes, focuses his mind, and forms a message for her: *Nothing so much enhances a good as to make sacrifices for it.*

As Jud checks Allsun for message received, the lab trailer hatch flies open and Guy lowers himself inside. "Heard from Conrad. Any break in the weather and he's on his way out." Stepping from the chair, he asks, "How they doing?"

Jud consciously remakes his face to suit the role of nursemaid. "Allsun seems to be coming around."

Guy immediately bends to her, checking her pulse. "Really?"

"Well, for a moment it looked like she was going to wake up." And accuse me, he thinks.

Guy takes his fingers away from her neck. "Yes, her heartbeat is regular . . . fast but regular." He shifts his attention to Neal. After a time, he mutters, "Not much change here."

He stands. Guy's eyes roam the trailer as if searching for something. He notices for the first time how cluttered the little trailer has become with bits of equipment, some of it in need of repair, tools, clothing, files, even a carton of toilet paper. It's an affront to his sense of order, but that's a luxury he can't afford right now. The empty food container on the counter brings his attention back to Jud. "You should get some sleep," he says to Jud. "We need a schedule." Guy's last statement hangs in the air while Jud zips his jacket and pulls on his hat and mitts. "A media schedule . . . Chuck Ford is in Churchill, ready to come out with Conrad."

Jud pauses at this news before stepping onto the chair and hoisting himself through the hatch.

Guy remarks to the disappearing body, "Ford's been in

town a couple of days checking out the rocket range."

Jud's face appears in the hatch, a ghost moon in an obscure sky. "What?"

"Ford's been looking over the abandoned rocket range outside Churchill for some project called Sixty Degrees North." Guy clears himself a space at the workbench and hands up the pack with Jud's breakfast dishes. "Conrad's been taking him around."

"Has Ford's crew arrived?" Jud speaks down the hole, wondering if he's going to miss his chance to get Chuck Ford alone.

"Don't know," Guy says. He is distracted, already listing the visiting media, counting beds, arranging shoots around his research. Jud is forgotten as the hatch door falls shut.

Guy concentrates on his schedule. Chuck Ford is first on site. There should always be a bed for Conrad in case he has to or wants to stay. Ford is bringing *Wild World*'s cameraman, soundman and director. Then there's the CBC filming David Suzuki and *The Nature of Things*, so two technicians and Suzuki in that group. Shit, the Tundra Buggy should have a revolving door. Oh, yeah, and Richard Rowan for *National Geographic*.

The media interest, considered timely, given the need to seek corporate funding, had nevertheless been a strain on resources: the hiring of a Tundra Buggy, for one thing. Normal research circumstances saw no more than four people at the Cape at one time, accommodated on two bunks and two folding army cots in the cramped tower hut.

The Cape Churchill research camp had been constructed to protect both people and bears, testimony to a philosophy of safety through removing temptation. To that end, a 45-foot steel observation tower had been built and anchored in the gravel on the shores of Hudson Bay. A steel storage cage and a steel observation cage at ground level were used to protect equipment, supplies and humans. The lab trailer, a box without wheels, had been brought in, raised off the ground and reinforced against curious bears. Polar bears were often found sleeping under the trailer out of the wind. And now the Tundra Buggy, a special bunkhouse on 1000-lb. tires that lift it twelve feet off the unforgiving rock of the Bay and beyond the reach of marauding bears.

When Guy had complained of the cost of renting the Tundra Buggy, Neal had reminded him it was a sign of success. Guy had culled years of research, his own and others', to produce a *Safety in Bear Country Reference Manual*. The manual, along with a bear safety program, had been so well received that Guy's department had gone on to distribute 450 *Safety in Bear Country Reference Manuals* throughout Canada, the United States and Northern Europe, and to set up workshops to train instructors. Now courses in bear-people conflict and safety were being offered through the Arctic College. Guy's education program was based on coexisting with bears. This year's research at the Cape would contribute more data toward polar bear detection and deterrence methods, allowing Guy to upgrade the manual.

Guy stares at the list of people coming and going. Certainly he's gratified, but he would rather be left alone with his bears. Totally alone.

He listens to the sound of Allsun's and Neal's shattered breath. Somewhere below their faltering rhythm, he can hear bears scratching and snuffling under the trailer. Other days, alone in the lab trailer, he has listened to the bears below the floor, registering their ticks, grumbles and dreams. They sound not unlike his dogs sleeping under the kitchen table. Perhaps all creatures resemble each other in sleep, only in sleep. Shamans understand this. In trance they follow Nanuk to the horizon where lines erase and words are the only prey.

Guy's affinity for the white bear has survived Jane Martin's death. He looks down at Neal, who, he is sure, would not care to know that Guy blames Jane, not the bear. And, of course, Neal blames Guy. He closes his eyes to this thought, and he sees it again, clearly: Jane's body. Neal is lying in the same place on the trailer floor where they had rested her body five years ago.

Why in God's name hadn't she heard the bear?

Perhaps in the long hours spent in the lab trailer bent over microscope and data sheets, she had just got used to the sound of the bears under the trailer floor. She slept little, so intense was her focus, her dedication. Jane worked on a whole different level. She was of the school that professed women had to work twice as hard as men to succeed.

Then, there was the stress of her relationship with Neal. They were lovers. A professor involved with her student, she had a lot to lose. Moral turpitude was expected of the old boys of the academy. But of a woman professor? The double standard that made adultery possible generally was alive and well in the enlightened ivory tower.

Jane must have had a lot on her mind. That he could understand. What was beyond him was how she seemed to have forgotten where she was. How could her senses have let her down, and him? Guy, in moments like these, admitted his own losses: his friendship with Neal altered, a mentor lost, a magnificent animal dead by his hand.

Afterwards, when he had taken the job with Renewable Resources and moved to Inuvik, Guy told himself he would make the kind of difference that would honour his dead. It sounded right as he flew toward the midnight sun. But this high sentiment lost its luster as the sun went out and he settled into long, dark days of office work.

It was friendship that set the balance right. Guy made friends among the native elders who use Inuvik as home base. What he had felt at Cape Churchill, they understood and gave meaning in ritual. But first there were stories of hunting, of sharing food, of dancing and then of *innua*—the souls of animals.

Later, Guy realized that his new friends, from the very moment he told them he had shot a polar bear at the Cape, were leading him to do the right thing. The elders consider Nanuk a being of infinite wisdom, in communication with a spirit world. They described the "village of the spirit bears" way out on the ice. He, Guy, must show his respect for his dead bear's *innua*, his soul.

They lent Guy a bear skin that he was to hang in his living room. He was to place on the floor below it the finest knives and tools he owned. For four days he was to do no work, remaining constantly in the presence of the bear.

Where an elder would have provided the bear with a crooked knife and a bone drill, to prove himself a "reliable man," Guy offered a stainless steel carving knife and a Phillips screwdriver. To honor the bear, he took two vacation days, adding them to a weekend.

There he sat with the Gwich'in elders, while friends came and went making pot after pot of strong tea. He had wished he still smoked.

There was much to learn about sitting. It wasn't about posture; it was about stillness. Gradually it dawned on him that they were stalking his bear's spirit. Stillness is at the heart of the polar bear. At a seal hole, a polar bear can remain motionless for hours, days if need be. Guy was honoring the essence of the white bear.

He had ranged far and wide in those four days, covering as much inner geography as polar bears cover physical terrain. Only a great wanderer knows stillness. This he was told and had to accept, since his experience with quietude was connected to place, to rootedness. For him it was a milking stool in a cow barn at sunrise, or above the world in a fire tower glued to a pair of long-distance eyes. Guy had resolved to spend time out on the pack ice, wandering among the pressure ridges—the plate tectonics of the Beaufort Sea thrusting up ice mountains—the home of the polar bear.

In tracking the soul of his polar bear, Guy had also been making his way toward Jane's. After four days, the spirit bear might consider him a reliable man, but he doubted Jane's *innua* would. He had let her down; recrimination was all he found.

GUY AWAKENS TO pain. His head is thrown back, so the hard back-rail of the chair presses into the base of his skull like a medieval instrument of torture. Sound echoes in the trailer. He must have been snoring. With lucidity comes the realization: he's hearing a chopper. He leaps up, only to crumple, plummeting toward Allsun's outstretched arm. Catching himself, he holds onto the counter, propped up so the blood can return to his right leg. He endures the agony of bloodrush with clenched teeth. Damn, damn! He needs to load the shotgun and get out there.

By the time Guy makes the launching pad, Jud, shotgun in hand, is escorting Conrad Cain and a man in an oversized red eiderdown jacket to the tower. Guy scans the camp for bears, calling a greeting and alerting Jud to the fact he has backup. It is only as they start to climb the ladder below him that he notices the weather. The storm has abated somewhat, but it is still a hummer. And Conrad has flown out. He doesn't know whether to be relieved or pissed off. Then he notices the evacuation baskets attached to the skids of the Bell 206 Jet Ranger. Guy settles for relieved.

"Conrad, you ballsy son-of-a-bitch. What're you doing out in this weather?" Guy claps Conrad's gloved hand with his own bare, reddening paw.

"Sightseeing. Showing Mr. Ford, here, around." Conrad steps carefully to one side on the crowded platform so he can introduce Chuck Ford, who has struck a rigid pose, his teeth chattering despite the ski jacket.

Guy motions to the Tundra Buggy. "Let's get out of the wind."

Single file, with Jud in the lead scouting under the gangplank for bears—specters in the swirling snow—they cross to the Buggy's deck, through the propped-open door and inside.

"Whoa, what y'all been doing?" Chuck is backing up toward the open door.

"Propane leak." Jud's tone is perfunctory.

"Dangerous," is Chuck Ford's single-word reply as he studies Jud. Ford's eyes are twin lights down the tunnel of his jacket hood.

Conrad looks around. "Where are the others?"

Yes, the "others," Guy thinks. Conrad the Calm, he's not here for the "victims" or "patients" or "evacuees," just the other Cape dwellers. "In the lab trailer," Guy says.

Conrad sees a problem. "The door to that thing still boarded up?"

"Yeah, the door's covered, Boris spikes and all, but we . . ."

"And they're unconscious, right?" Conrad is distracted, working out what it's going to take to get Neal and Allsun out of the trailer and into the baskets.

"Jud and I got them in, the four of us can get them out."

"Okay, let's do it." Conrad turns to the door, but Guy is already on the Tundra Buggy deck checking for bears.

The four of them cross the gangplank that vibrates with their steps and arrive on the tower platform that flexes in the middle with their weight.

Guy leads the way onto the lab trailer roof. He and Conrad shimmy down the hatch, leaving Jud and Chuck above. Conrad assesses his new passengers, mentally calculating their individual and combined weights, while Guy checks their pulses, breathing, and the color of lips and fingers.

"We should zip them into those sleeping bags." Conrad bends to the task. "It's going to be colder than a mother-in-law's kiss flying in those baskets. Pull their toques down around their faces."

"Shit, you're right. I hadn't ..." Guy stands and shouts up the hatch, "Jud, my backpack in the Tundra Buggy, there's a couple of balaclavas. Get 'em, okay?"

"Good," Conrad remarks. "That'll make the difference, even with the sleeping bags done up over their heads."

Once Allsun and Neal are wrapped against a wind chill that will reduce the temperature around the Plexiglas-covered baskets to below recording, they become extremely slippery, seemingly boneless bundles. The two men are hard-pressed to get a grip, let alone hoist the now upright Allsun through the hatch and into the waiting arms of Jud and Chuck.

Finally, they wrestle her onto the roof, across the platform, and down the tower ladder. Once in the basket, she is covered with additional sleeping bags and a space blanket.

Neal presents an even heavier challenge and Guy wonders, as the four of them hurry back to the tower, about Chuck Ford. Guy is not entirely sure what's under that huge jacket, but Ford is not a tall man and he seems paunchy. In trying to decide how much muscle is under Chuck's heavy clothes, Guy remembers that Ford is from New Orleans. He whistles through his teeth at this thought. The man must be freezing his balls off up here!

It's tougher going with Neal, and Guy notices that Jud is working hard to make up for a flagging partner in Ford. Where he expects to see some hint of disgust on his assistant's face, Guy detects self-satisfaction in Jud's eyes. Is this simply the attitude of a young man for one older? Or, perhaps, the host of *Wild World*'s reputation precedes him? Jud and Chuck had been talking while he and Conrad had been suiting Allsun and Neal up for their flight, but Guy had registered the sound of their voices, not their words.

Jud stands guard as Conrad and Guy check the baskets one last time. Satisfied, Conrad gets into the cockpit. The others run for the tower as the rotor blades whip frenzied snow into smoke and mirrors. They pause on the tower platform to catch their breath, all eyes watching Conrad levitate Allsun and Neal off the ground encased in their glass baskets. They disappear behind a white curtain.

Guy hopes Chuck has enough left in him to climb the tower to the hut. Thirty-three feet can seem like thirty-three hundred when you're not used to climbing ladders. He turns to the new arrival and motions upward. "Jud will lead the way and I'll be right behind you." Guy watches as Chuck leans back, tilting his hood so he can see how far he has to climb. The expression on Chuck's face tells Guy this isn't going to be a stroll. "The tower hut's heated and there's a stove for tea," Guy says by way of encouragement.

Chuck rallies. It's slow going, but they make it up without incident. In the tower hut, Ford keeps the mega-jacket on and zipped, his only concession to promised warmth the throwing off of his hood. Guy and Jud are presented with a red nose and cheeks mottled with white patches of frostbite.

"Chuck, how warm are your hands?" Guy asks.

"Fuckin' frozen." Chuck shoots him a look.

"Jud'll put on the kettle." He glances at Jud. "But in the meantime you should let me blow on your cheeks."

"What the hell?"

Guy catches the big grin on Jud's face as he lifts the kettle to gauge how much water is in it. Facing Guy, Chuck has his back to Jud and reads nothing but seriousness in a man he has known until now only as a name, Dr. Guy Thorpe, Ph.D., in correspondence with the Canadian government.

"You've got a couple of patches of frostbite on your cheeks. We should warm the skin up, get the circulation back . . . sooner than later." Guy takes off his gloves and chafes his own cold hands.

"Oh." Chuck rubs at his face. His mitts make him clumsy.

Guy is reminded of when he and his brother had chicken pox as kids; their mother had tied outsized leather mittens to their hands to keep them from scratching and scarring.

"Rubbing makes it worse. Tissue damage . . . frozen water crystals grind between the cells . . . Here . . ." Guy cups his own hands and blows through them on to one blanched spot, then the other, warming it gently with his breath. His actions are so quick and unassuming that Chuck has no opportunity to refuse.

Chuck looks everywhere but at Guy, who is too close for comfort. Guy steps back to assess his handiwork; Chuck breaks away, flopping down on one of the bunks. "This where we sleep?" he asks.

"Yeah." Guy studies Chuck, aware of some kind of disapproval, and the lack of a thank you for his first aid. "The researchers do."

"And the rest of us? I got three crew coming out." Chuck frowns down into the cup of tea Jud has handed him.

For a moment Jud is perplexed. "Oh, you need white death?"

"What?" Now Chuck is frowning and squinting up at Jud.

"Sugar or creamer." Jud is frowning right back.

Guy is aware of the two men sizing each other up. He is about to speak when Chuck unzips his jacket and extracts a flask from an inside pocket. Gripping the cap with his teeth, in one fluid motion he pops the stopper and pours a slug into his tea. He glances up, the gold-topped cork stuck in the side of his mouth like some gilded stogie, then offers up the flask. "Tennessee Wild Turkey. Make a man out of a man."

Jud isn't buying.

Guy accepts the flask; his mother didn't raise a foolish boy, or an impolite one. "The Tundra Buggy's for visitors."

Chuck swallows fast in order to speak. "That school bus reeking of gas?"

"Got eight bunks, closets, cooking counter. Hardly a school bus. We'll fix the propane heater today."

"Yeah." Chuck looks from Guy to Jud.

"It's not rocket science." Jud pours himself another cup of tea.

"More like bomb making." Chuck busies himself filling his empty tea mug with fortification.

Guy resolves to change the subject. "As soon as the storm lets up, we'll prepare the bait site, bring some polar bears in. We've still got lots of work to do."

"What do y'all mean by 'bring some polar bears in'?" Chuck lies back on the bunk, propping himself up against the unpainted plywood wall. His jacket slides open, confirming Guy's hunch that Chuck's gut is bigger than his chest.

Guy makes himself as comfortable as he can on a wooden chair, probably recycled from some government waiting room. "There are twenty-five polar bears, more or less, roaming this area waiting for freeze-up on the Bay. They tend to stay out on the spit watching the water turn to ice, conserving energy. Not much to eat around here ..."

"Cubs, maybe," Jud interjects. He's leaning against the door as if he is ready to leave.

Chuck nods at Guy. "No bears in camp?"

"They come and go. Especially the young ones—adolescents, and mothers with this year's cubs. They're hungrier than the adult males, who tend to hang out at the edge of the Bay. The young often lose their kills or scavenged meals to bigger bears. The females have been denned-up giving birth, feeding the cubs. They're down to skin and bone. They sleep under the trailer, the Tundra Buggy, in snow drifts under the gangplank, the tower. You got to watch out for them."

"Okay, so how do we get around? How do we film? I want this to go quick. It's too fucking cold up here to be pissing around ..."

"Carefully," Jud says, putting his mug upside down on the counter. He pauses at the door to put on his woolen gloves, the only pieces of clothing he had removed while in the hut, and says to Guy, "I'll be in the lab trailer."

"First rule," Guy leans forward in the chair, directing his unwavering gaze at Chuck, "no one, I repeat, no one goes to ground alone. You want to go to the can, you tell us. One of us will come along with a shot gun, the other will cover you from the launching pad."

"The what?" Chuck breaks Guy's fixed stare.

"The plywood platform between the tower legs."

"No." Chuck spits out the small word, his disgust punctuated by a spray of bourbon-fetid spittle. "The can? The can's outside?"

"Yeah, but it's okay. It's in the steel storage cage."

"That makes it *okay*? It must be a hundred below out there."

Guy notes the flush on Chuck's face. "Actually, it sounds like the storm's backing off." He gets up to check the thermometer mounted outside the plate glass window that fills the space above the counter. "Right on. It's up two degrees. Minus thirty Celsius."

"What's that in real talk?"

"Real? Oh, yeah sure, about minus twenty degrees F . . . Fahrenheit." Guy rubs his hands together. "I should give you a safety tour."

"What I'd really like," Chuck's eyes are closed, "is forty winks." He slides down into his jacket and is gone.

"Sure," Guy says. Sleep it off, is what he thinks. That's all I'd need, is you falling down the tower ladder.

Guy takes the binoculars down from the peg by the door and focuses out the window above the bunk on which Chuck lies snoring.

Where the landscape beyond the double pane picture window was a whiteout this morning, there is definition. But still not what Guy knows it to be—the esker refining itself into a sandspit before it reaches the tidal flats and the Bay. From rock to sand to water. All the ingredients by which *real* time can be measured.

Guy looks away and glances down at his boorish guest. He wonders just what kind of man he has allowed to come to this special place and disrupt his work. Any human venturing out here should be tranquilized, have a tag attached to his ear, a tooth pulled, a number tattooed on the inside of his lip, be measured, weighed and have a blood sample taken. The bears belong here and they suffer our desire to know about them, to classify, scrutinize, analyze. More than the same rigor should be applied to the likes of Chuck Ford before they ever set foot on this numinous soil.

BY EARLY AFTERNOON the wind-driven snow has abated. Guy has collected Chuck Ford from the tower hut and got him as far as the platform. They've stopped so Chuck can recover his sang-froid after slipping on the tower ladder, and Guy can check his own left hand. Chuck had insisted on coming down the ladder two-footed—put left foot on lower rung, put right foot on same rung, pause, repeat. Awkward, inefficient, made for an accident on icy steel. Halfway down Chuck's feet went out from under him and when Guy reached up to guide Chuck's feet back onto the rung, he got his hand stepped on for the effort. Nothing broken, Guy decides, flexing his fingers, but bruising for sure.

Chuck looks spooked as he eyes the last twelve feet of ladder, so Guy redirects his guest's attention. "See out there to the north." Guy points. " That's the bait site. It's surrounded by an electrified fence. We're testing the fence as a detection and deterrence device. Got an alarm hooked up to it, and a high voltage charge running through it, 12,000 V, but low amperage for safety."

"Whose safety?"

Guy studies Chuck, trying to understand what the man is asking. "You weren't planning on sampling its effectiveness, were you, Chuck? Give you a real nasty surprise. Bears are better insulated. So far we've found that between their well-furred paws and the dry, frozen soil, they're too well grounded to get much of a zap. Unless they connect with their nose or tongue."

"What are those stakes out there?" Chuck gestures toward the painted markers driven into the tundra, now askew after the blizzard.

"They mark the twenty-meter zones we use to clock the approach and exit rates of the bears. The markers encircle the camp." Guy points, his arm inscribing an arc in the air. "It's kind of like a big target with the bait site as the bull's eye." Guy massages the fingers of his bruised hand until he notices Chuck watching. Pulling on his wool gloves, he continues, "We record how fast the bears respond to the scent of food and how quickly they're driven away by the fence, say, or by Ferret slugs, Bear Thumpers, Cart-a-balls, Screamers, Rocket Bangers . . . we got a whole deterrence arsenal we're testing. And this year for the first time we're trying out Red Pepper Spray."

"So you're saying we should be shooting the bait site for this footage?" Chuck looks around. "From where?"

"Not ground level. There'll be bears all over camp. So you could film from here, or the Tundra Buggy deck, or the trailer roof."

"Shit, I don't know." Chuck is shaking his head, making his jacket hood bob like a red buoy. "We're going to get backs, the fucking tops of heads."

Guy is beginning to lose patience. It's time Chuck got a grip on just what he's dealing with here. "Looks like Jud's nearly ready to set out the bait. Tell you what, for this session we'll put you in the one-man observation cage . . . see what you think."

Chuck steps to the edge of the plywood platform to get a good look at the observation cage.

Guy puts a hand on Chuck's arm. "Step back, please."

"What?"

"Back. Back from the edge." Guy applies pressure. "See that gouge?" He points to a 2 x 4 cross-member acting as a railing. "Made by a claw. Standing on his hind legs, a good-size male can reach up here, get a paw on the perimeter. You won't necessarily see him. They're smart enough to come up from under the platform, rather than directly at you. Polar bears understand the element of surprise."

"Holy hell, you said we're twelve feet off the ground here . . ." There's a question in Chuck's voice. "You're not joshing me, now are you?"

"Had a photographer shooting from up here on the platform last year. He's focused on the bait site, but there's a bear below him. They're both ignoring each other, when the bear leaps onto fuel drums stored beside the tower and from there lunges at the photographer. Tore the man's pant-leg open before falling to the ground."

"Smart bastard, huh?"

"Don't underestimate them. A male bear can be five or six feet at the shoulder. It's like standing next to a horse. Except a polar bear sees you as just another meal . . . a seal in a ski jacket."

"My crew's experienced." Chuck is still not convinced this is the best shooting site.

"Good. Unless they want to try from up the tower or the deck of the Tundra Buggy, the launching pad is the best I can offer." Guy wants it understood that there'll be no foolishness, no taking chances.

"Launching pad?" Chuck has heard the warning and is now downplaying the imperative.

"It's what we started calling the platform after Phil the photographer was nearly launched into the hereafter." Guy notices Jud pick up the shotgun he has with him in the storage cage and turn to them. "Jud's ready," he says to Chuck. Guy ventures to the edge and leans out over the scored cross-member, checking under the launching pad, sweeping under the lab trailer to his left, Tundra Buggy and gangplank to his right with a practiced gaze. He counts on Jud to protect him as he does this reconnaissance. To Chuck he says, "Let's make it fast," as he starts down the ladder.

But Chuck isn't fast and Guy finds himself waiting at the bottom of the tower ladder without a gun for protection. He sprints to the storage cage. Jud hands him the shotgun. Guy scrutinizes the camp carefully, cursing under his breath. Finally, Chuck makes it to the ground and Guy hustles him along.

It's crowded in the steel storage cage. There are empty crates, fuel drums, and axes for cutting holes in the ice on a nearby pothole lake that provides fresh water. There are crowbars, shovels, rolled tarps, and a wooden toilet seat.

Jud collects a crowbar and directs Chuck with a wave of the bar. "Could you slide over by the toilet, give me some room?"

Chuck looks around.

"The blue drum." Guy points to a small oil drum behind Chuck. "That's the camp toilet."

"Ah-huh."

Jud applies the crowbar to the rim of the orange bait drum. He pops and removes the lid in one quick motion. The stench is staggering.

"It's like removing a band-aid," Jud says. "It's more painful by degrees."

Guy reassures Chuck, who looks as if he's going to retch. "Now that you've got a snoutful, your olfactory nerves will burn out . . . it won't be so bad." Looking to Jud as a fellow Canadian for confirmation, Guy offers up a comparison, "Not much different from running over a skunk on the highway."

"Seal and beluga," Jud explains as he uses a pair of barbecue tongs to lift out a hunk of reeking flesh. "Marinated in whale oil and horse fat."

"Ten Dead Horses," Guy takes up the explanation. "Commercial predator-lure." He slips the lid back on the bait drum while Jud reaches for a mesh contraption, laying it on top of the orange lid.

Jud slaps the piece of meat between two small squares cut from chain link fencing and hinged together with wire on one side. With his bare fingers wielding the pliers, he wires the whale sandwich shut on the other three sides.

Chuck's eyes are streaming, the tears freezing on his eyelashes and cheeks. It's obvious he's not going to remove his hands from where they cover his nose and mouth to wipe away the tears.

Jud picks up the mesh sandwich with the tongs and

reaches for the shotgun with his free hand. As he turns, the reeking mess dribbles over one of Chuck's boots.

A strangled cry comes from behind Chuck's mitt as he contemplates the shiny slash of rank oil over the rubberized toe of his pristine SnowPaks.

"It's a bit tight in here," Jud says to Chuck, as he follows Guy out of the storage cage.

Guy latches the door behind Chuck. "We're going out to the bait site, so keep your eyes peeled." Guy unslings the Winchester from his shoulder and shifts it to a two-handed carry.

They pass the lab trailer with its boarded-up door.

"Shit, look at that!" Chuck whistles through his teeth.

"What?" Guy asks sharply, following Chuck's gaze.

"All those spikes."

"Oh." Guy sounds relieved. "You mean Boris's iron maiden. Keeps the bears from ripping off the plywood cover." They walk on. "Old Boris Oszurkiewicz in Churchill came up with this little trick of banging eight-inch spikes right through three-quarter-inch plywood, two inches apart all up and down, and using the armored plywood to board up his doors and windows."

They cover the ground to the bait site quickly, passing the target markers at measured intervals. As they approach the electrified fence, Guy points out a solar panel mounted on a twelve-volt Gel battery. "That's our source for charging the fence. The wires are live, so be careful."

The bear barbecue is inside the fence. They've converted an empty oil barrel to this purpose by laying it on its side, and filling it half full of gravel. Resting on the gravel inside the drum is a cast-iron frying pan laden with glowing charcoal briquettes. Jud drops the bait sandwich on the outside of the barrel.

Guy bends down to look in the open end of the barrel and motions to Chuck to do the same. "We heat the briquettes on the Coleman stove, otherwise they won't light. It's too cold out here." He gets a grunt of agreement from Chuck. "Once they get going, it's enough to heat the wall of the barrel. And you got yourself a barbecue."

Chuck straightens, stamping his feet in spite of his canvas and felt boots. "Christ, that's at least a fifty-gallon drum, why all the gravel?"

"So it's harder for the bears to toss around." Jud answers from where he is prodding the briquettes with the barbecue tongs.

"You're kidding?"

"Never kid about bears." Jud uses the same tongs to flip over the bait.

Guy scans the willow-covered esker beyond where they stand inside a flimsy fence, attempting to lure the largest land predator in the world. He shakes his head at the thought.

Chuck stamps his feet some more and eyes the one-man observation cage off to one side of the barbecue.

"We should start back." Guy has detected activity on the Bayside horizon. "You're welcome to stay out, Chuck. Did you bring your camera? Incredible shots from inside the observation cage."

Chuck hugs himself to capture what little warmth there is in his jacket. He surreptitiously pats the flask in his breast pocket. "Yeah, I'll stay," he says. Jud swings open the door of the six-by-six-foot steel observation cage and Chuck enters.

"Stay in the center. Keep your hands and anything else away from the bars. Do not try to attract the bears to you. That'll mess up our data." Jud has Chuck secure the latch on the inside, then Jud grabs the bars with both hands and shakes the door, putting his weight into it.

Jud joins Guy back at the lab trailer, where they assemble the data sheets, deterrence guns and dye bottles, as they wait for the bears to come in to the bait site and trigger the alarm attached to the electrified fence. In their experience they have enough time to chart which methods will be used: Phase one—scare cartridges fired from pistols using .22 caliber blanks; Phase two—non-lethal projectiles fired from a Mod 267 Smith Wesson gas and flare gun, a Winchester 870 open bore shotgun, and a rubber bullet Riot Gun.

When the alarm bell sounds in the lab trailer, they're ready. Carrying their equipment, Guy and Jud make their way to the launching pad.

"No new ones out there," Jud remarks.

"Give me the identifiers. I'll record them." Guy takes up his clipboard and pencil.

"Okay, we got three marked by Wildlife Services . . . HM, YA, and XT, all males. Two marked with our Bear Thumpers. Geez, we got another male marked with one of our Ferret slugs and a Cart-a-ball. Glutton for punishment. No dye jobs."

"How's Chuck doing?" Guy concentrates on checking off boxes on the data sheet.

"Behaving himself. The bears have made a beeline for the barbecue. Not interested in him. Probably his after-shave . . . eau de bourbon."

Guy glances up at Jud, surprised at his wit. To date, his

assistant has shown next to no sense of humor. "Alright, so we've got repeat offenders. Let's see what kind of exit times we get out of them." Guy takes a stopwatch from his pocket.

"Hold on. There's an unmarked female and cub below us." Jud opens a tool box and takes out a plastic squeeze bottle of Burgundy Babe hair dye. He checks under the platform for other bears. Sure that he's not being stalked, he leans out and writes a number six on the white back of the passing bear. She responds to the expiration of the squeeze bottle with a languid turn of her head. She's the predator. She has no natural enemies. Man, the unnatural enemy, she views as a curiosity. What concerns her is getting in on the food while keeping her cub safe from the males.

"Okay." Jud is back with Guy in the center of the launching pad. "Since she's new in town, I'll record her response to the scare cartridges."

Guy raises what looks like a six-shooter toward the sky and fires off a Banger. A spiraling tail of light marks its path for seventy-five feet before it explodes with a loud bang over top of the bait-site bears. Chuck, startled, stumbles against the back wall of the cage, but not one bear misses a step in the intricate dance of dominance around the smoking barbecue. The response is the same for the Screamer and the Whistle, screeching through the sky from the time they're popped off. Either the commotion or the open-mouth, hissing roars coming from the males has encouraged the dyed female to take her cub in under the lab trailer.

One of the males has made a move. With graceful control, he has hooked the whale sandwich off the barbecue. He's not sure how to unwrap this tidbit; one swipe of a claw tears open a seal's skin. But this won't have him puzzled for long, if he manages to keep it.

"We better get on them. They're not going to stay long now the bait's taken." Guy hands Jud a Smith Wesson with a custom barrel of standard steel Dom and Aim-point sight. "Take out one of the peripheral males." Guy has loaded the gun with seventy-five grains of black powder, a Federal 209 primer, and a Bear Thumper Liquid Slug—a soft plastic casing filled with dye.

Jud aims for the rump. Hit, the bear skitters sideways, turns and trots through the electrified fence. "Damn. Another repair job to that friggin' fence."

Guy looks from the zone markers the retreating bear is passing to the stopwatch, and records. He gives Jud the watch and goes for the Winchester with its three-slug load. "I'll work my way from the outside bears to the male with the sandwich. First shot: Cart-a-ball." The shotgun is mounted with rifle sights and in this case Guy aims for the front right shoulder of the bear facing him. A hit. The bear sways its head as if to shake off the sting of a black fly and backs away. There is a round shoe polish mark on his fur where the ball has connected. Despite the direct hit, the male is not leaving.

"Second shot, same candidate, Ferret slug," Guy announces. The bear has turned back to the meal. Guy shoots him in the rump. The hard plastic projectile has him dancing away from the barbecue. He decides he's had enough of this party.

"Third shot, Ferret slug." Guy displaces another bait-site bear, noting that none of them leaves at any great pace. With Ferret slugs they seem to keep their dignity intact. "Let's go to the Riot Gun for the big male hogging lunch."

Jud raises the 38-mm single shot to his shoulder, settles it close against the recoil. He gives the trigger a firm, long squeeze. A sound louder than the crack of a high-powered rife heralds an unpredicted spectacle. The polar bear, struck in the shoulder, rises with electric speed into a standing position, front paws jabbing the air like a shadow boxer. The bear spots his opponent.

Ears flat against his skull, the bear drops and charges the observation cage. Rearing up again, he slams the cage with the force of his nine hundred pounds of muscle and attitude.

The cage rocks. Chuck struggles to maintain his balance.

The bear gives the cage a shove, testing to see what it will take to break the barrier between him and his perceived antagonist.

Standing above the cage, he brings his mighty paws down hard on the roof, the same technique he would use to pound in the roof of a snow cave to scoop a seal pup from its birth lair.

Guy aims the backup shotgun containing kill loads, while Jud reloads the Riot Gun. "Okay, Jud. Do it."

Guy blinks at the report from the Riot Gun and in the same moment prays that the hard rubber baton will move the big male off, not enrage him more. He honestly doesn't know just how much of this kind of abuse 2.5-inch angle iron slats welded and bolted to a steel frame can take. He's prepared to offer the bear mere seconds to make up its mind. Guy will have no choice but to shoot to kill.

The bear whirls as if executing a pirouette. The rubber baton has struck him in the rib cage, a vital area. It's a potentially lethal hit.

Guy holds his breath as the bear staggers. The moaning sound the polar bear makes distresses Guy as much as the cries of an injured baby would.

The bear regains his balance, turns and retreats. His gait suggests to Guy that he's not too badly injured. Guy is hoping the tough hide and hard muscle of this resilient animal have protected its bones and internal organs from damage.

Jud reloads the Winchester.

Scouting the whole camp, Guy is particularly careful to check under the lab trailer for number six and her cub. The camp is clean; the curious bears have been driven away by the alarmed cries of the big male.

The men go to ground. With as much speed as caution allows, they approach the bait site, the cage and Chuck.

ONCE IN THE lab trailer, Chuck gets the shakes. They are so bad he gives up on the cup and swigs Wild Turkey straight from the bottle. There was no way he was able to climb to the tower hut. It was more than enough climbing the ladder to the platform and then having to come down through that rabbit hole in the trailer roof. "Jesus H. Christ with a crutch, why did y'all wait so long to shoot that fucking bear?"

Guy turns away from Chuck. "You hear that?" he asks Jud.

"Yeah, a chopper." Jud reaches for one of the shotguns, hands it to Guy, and gets the other for himself.

Guy approaches Chuck slumped on the chair under the hatch, but Chuck doesn't move. "Chuck, can you shift to the stool in the corner? We need the chair to get out." Guy doesn't hide his impatience.

"This is turning out to be a real trip." Chuck's drawl only heightens the sarcasm in his voice.

Left alone, he sizes up the lab trailer, and decides there is no way the flimsy walls would keep a polar bear out.

Laughter cuts through the plywood and tin of Chuck's contemplation. Laughing . . . a laugh he recognizes. His crew has arrived. Lord be praised!

Hal Bienville, Pete Paul and Lucas Clark are joking about their armed guard as they climb the tower ladder to the platform. Hal, originally from New Orleans, is no stranger to firepower and expects it in the Louisiana bayous, but not in the Canadian barrens. A tall man, who has drawn his dark good looks from the French, Spanish and Caribbean heritage of his city, is being teased by Pete for what he calls a typical lack of knowledge. Pete is short and dark with a smooth-skin innocence that masks a sharp wit. His childhood nickname is Mink, after a mischievous character in his grandfather's stories. Lucas simply smiles his quiet smile. His angular Ichabod Crane body belies a steady strength.

The hatch opens and a familiar face peers down at Chuck. "Hey guys, it's Quinn the Eskimo—"

"You're fired, Pete."

"Good day to you too, Mr. Ford, sir."

Pete the cameraman is replaced by Hal the director. "Chuck, how you doing? They just told us—"

"Get me out of this goddamn hole." Chuck attempts

to stand on the chair. It wobbles and sways. He goes limp and slides down to a sitting position.

"I'll come down. Can you move off the chair? Chuck?" Hal spots the bottle of Wild Turkey. "Ah shit. Chuck, get off the damned chair."

Chuck stares at the floor and waits, listening. Silence. Enough to irritate Hal even more. Then, with unexpected speed, Chuck leaps up on the chair, shouting, "It's under there!" He sways dangerously. "Get me out, get me out!"

Hal, thinking Chuck is into another round of the DT's, reaches down. "Grab on, Chuck," he commands.

Once Hal has steadied Chuck, he realizes the man down the hole is dead weight, or near to it. And too short to get his elbows up and over the rim of the hatch to lever himself out. "Chuck, I'm going to come down." Hal's tone is meant to reassure. There is no way he can haul Chuck's bulk up by his arms.

"No, the floor. It'll hear." Chuck's thinks he's whispered these words. But it's no whisper, just a shrill whine.

Still grasping Chuck's arms, Hal swings him like a sack of hammers and then lets go. Chuck falls off the chair. Hal turns his lanky frame around and is backing down the hatch before Chuck can right himself. Hal and Lucas exchange a look that speaks to how bone-weary they both are of Chuck's idiosyncrasies. Hal and Lucas are old hands at handling Chuck Ford, but it doesn't seem to get any easier.

Chuck looks up at Hal wide-eyed. "Under the floor ... there's a bear."

"Okay, so let's get out of here. I'll boost you up, Pete

and Lucas will pull you through." Hal bends over Chuck. "Here, take my hand."

This is more easily said than done. Chuck's girth, padded with heavy clothing—he's like a stopper, a cork that's been pushed down the neck of a wine bottle. Finally, when Hal puts his shoulder hard into Chuck's butt and heaves, it's enough to pop Chuck up to where the rest of the crew can grab him under the arms and haul him out.

Pete rests a minute, although he's not as winded as Lucas the soundman appears to be. Pete reasons that it's because he lives humping his heavy cameras around that he's not breathing as hard as Lucas is. In a deep, slow, mimicking drawl, Pete says to no one in particular, "More fun than wrestling a catfish away from an alligator."

From the platform, Jud watches Chuck's delivery. He thinks about polar bears pulling seals through their small breathing holes in the ice with such force that the seal is reduced to a skin bag full of broken bones. Chuck looks up at him from where he is lying on the trailer roof. Jud grins.

Guy joins Jud. "Think we'll get him up the ladder to the hut?"

"No choice." Jud continues to look on.

"We got Allsun up the tower alright. Put her and Richard Rowan between Conrad and me. Took it slow." Guy watches as Hal surfaces. Even though his schedule has changed yet again, Guy is glad to see Chuck's people. Perhaps they can take Ford in hand, get the shoot done and get out. That went for Richard Rowan as well. Not that he has anything against the man. In fact, Rowan climbed the tower ladder with confidence and was quick to help Allsun when she faltered. It didn't look as if

Rowan would need baby-sitting, but Allsun might. Apparently she hadn't inhaled as much of the propane as Neal had; her bunk had been further away from the furnace. But she wasn't as well as she claimed. Her miraculous recovery had more to do with sheer pig-headedness.

"Thought Chuck's crew and this Richard Rowan weren't due in Churchill till tomorrow." Jud is marveling at how the Philistines have materialized in the wilderness of Cape Churchill. The best-laid schemes …

"So did I. Ford's people heard the weather was coming in up here, so they chartered a plane. Rowan spotted them at the Winnipeg airport." Guy motions the others to come over to the platform. They must be freezing their butts off; he knows he is. "I wish Allsun had stayed in the hospital. At least overnight. She looks like hell."

"Speaking of night, where's everyone going to sleep?" Jud stands statue-like, intent.

Guy has noticed his assistant doesn't do the shift and stomp, the dance of the north practiced by those required to stop in the cold. It's as if he's testing himself against the elements. "As soon as we get these people upstairs, we're going to fix the propane furnace in the Tundra Buggy. Conrad brought me in a new valve."

IT TAKES GUY and Jud a while to figure out how to get the old valve off and the new one on. The Tundra Buggy is like a deep freeze, holding in the cold but seemingly not the gas. Their exposed fingers become white with cold. Their eyes don't tear—a good sign.

When they're set to replace the propane tank, Jud

takes the shotgun and from the Tundra Buggy deck does a bear reconnaissance. To reach the tank strapped to the outside wall of the Buggy, Guy will have to climb down onto one of the ten-foot-high tires—within bear range. Jud is cautiously leaning out over the solid deck railing, checking for bears under the Tundra Buggy.

Ready to give Guy the all clear, Jud hears voices. He follows the sound to the landing outside the tower hut. Chuck is there, dragging on a cigarette. There is another man leaning against the wall off to one side and behind Chuck. At first Jud thinks it is Hal—tall, long-limbed—until he hears the man say, "I know everything." The accent is Bostonian; the voice belongs to Richard Rowan. He folds his arms across his chest. Chuck keeps his face turned away. Staring at the tip of his cigarette, he says, "I make nature films. What's to know?"

Before Richard can respond, Guy appears on the Tundra Buggy deck hefting the fresh propane tank. "We good?" he asks Jud.

Jud hesitates, reluctant to answer and miss what is being said on the tower landing above him. Chuck is speaking, but all Jud catches is the word "nothing." He shifts his attention to Guy. "Yeah."

Guy sets the tank on the deck. His hands free now, he lets himself down over the outside of the railing and swings onto the top of the tire. He steadies himself, all the while on the watch for bears, then reaches up and takes the tank Jud is lowering to him. Jud strains to hear the men on the tower landing, but his ears are full of Guy grunting the new tank into place.

Guy makes Jud wait outside while he lights the furnace. The task is made awkward by his attempt to keep his face turned away. Guy expels a long, held breath when the furnace emits the normal *pop* that signals it's lit. He leaves the Tundra Buggy door open a crack, just in case.

As Guy climbs the tower ladder he gets a whiff of something. It's not the familiar smell of cold—the scent of wet sheets on a clothesline. Guy hesitates, wondering if it's the propane furnace. Should he go back down? Then it hits him. Food! It's the smell of cooking, real cooking. It's been so long that he's forgotten the aroma of fresh meat, spices. Tonight there would be no tinny tang to set his fillings on edge, his mind awash with the color gray.

On the counter, Conrad has laid out a buffet. Jars and plastic containers are open, displaying contents not immediately recognizable. Guy is aware of the sweetish aroma of wild game mingled with the fetor of unwashed work clothes and the pervasive pong of seal oil from the bait barrel. The pong is coming from him and Jud, and a little from the baptized toe of Chuck's SnowPaks. The smell of seal oil is so offensive, even polar bears wash themselves fastidiously after dining on a seal kill.

Guy looks at Conrad and raises his eyebrows in an unspoken but saliva-forming question.

"My friend in Yellowknife. She's putting a cookbook together. Sends me the leftovers when she's trying out recipes. Convinced that a man without a wife will eat only potato chips . . . and beer." He chuckles. Conrad waves a hand at the laden counter. "My leftovers are your leftovers."

Pete the cameraman doesn't have to be asked twice. "What'cha got here? Smells like my auntie's cooking."

"Help yourself." Conrad hands Pete a tin plate.

The hut was never meant for a crowd. There's barely enough room for three people to stand at one time, so they go to the counter in shifts.

"Hey, man, this is moose, right?" Pete is the first to comment on what must be unfamiliar textures, let alone tastes, to most of Conrad's dinner guests. "Whoa, takes me right back to the bush."

"Moose, you say? Filmed them," Hal says. His fork screeches against the tin plate.

"Okay, so what else we got here?" Pete lifts a morsel, sniffs, puts it in his mouth. "Chews like fowl, but the barbecue sauce ... hides the wild bird taste. Going mostly on feel, my guess, this is grouse." He captures a different piece of dark meat. "And this is duck with Worcestershire sauce."

Conrad claps Pete on the shoulder. "How is it you know wild meat?"

"Got family on the Sliammon Reserve," Pete says as he chews.

"Where's that?" Conrad asks, as he helps himself to the food at last.

"West Coast, near Powell River." Pete glances at the counter to see what's left.

Hal chimes in, "One hundred and thirty-three kill-ah-meet-hers from Vancouver, British Columbia . . . as the raven flies." He studiously ignores Pete.

"So, what's this grouse thing?" Lucas is looking at his plate for clues.

"Prairie chicken where you come from," Pete obliges. "Nebraska must still have prairie chickens. You haven't blasted them out of existence, have you?"

"Hell, Pete, not everyone's a redneck," Lucas counters. "You been living too long in Louisiana."

"You keep a civil tongue in your head when speaking of my ancestral home." Hal points his fork at Lucas. "This duck?" There's a piece of meat on the end of the fork. "Unusual taste for duck."

"Some up-north ingenuity," Conrad allows. "The northerners I know have a fondness for HP Sauce."

"HP?" Hal asks with a drawl that turns two lonely consonants into a word complete with vowels.

"House of Parliament. Imported from England. Buy it by the case up north." Conrad sounds off-hand, but there's a look in his eye. "Dip their muktuk in it." He pauses, letting the word settle in.

"Whale blubber, eaten raw." Pete ups the ante in Conrad's game.

Both Hal and Lucas eye their plates. Conrad gets on with making tea. Pete goes back for seconds.

"So, Conrad, you always lived up here?" Hal changes the subject.

"Since '67. A Saskatchewan farm boy. 'Running from the plough.' My old man's words," Conrad says over his shoulder as he fills the kettle with water. "Probably right. Nothing growing, nothing grazing up here. Summer means monster mosquitoes and bears only slightly bigger." He lights a burner on the Coleman stove, sets the kettle to boil and turns to Hal.

"I wouldn't imagine there was much here back then?" Hal collects the empty plates and hands them over to Conrad.

"More than there is now. I came out here to work as a grain handler; funny, eh? You must've seen the grain elevators when you flew in. I figured I'd do that for a while, then sign on one of those freighters I was loading and see the world. Ended up training at Fort Churchill. That's where I learned to fly ..." The whistle on the kettle calls a time out as Conrad attends to the tea.

"Fort Churchill?" Lucas asks. "Saw those grain elevators. Recognized those right off. Didn't see any base."

"Nope, gone. The biggest joint Canadian/American military base in the world. Forty-five hundred servicemen, support staff, families ... it was bigger than the town of Churchill." Conrad starts handing around mugs of tea. "Had its own hospital, schools, movie theatre, the works. Both governments pulled the troops out in '64, then it was used for training, maneuvers, stuff like that. They bulldozed it in 1981." He pours the remainder of the hot water over the dirty dishes stacked in a plastic tub.

"So what did you—" Hal's question is punctuated by a profound snore coming from Chuck, who is slumped beside Hal on one of the bunks. When they turn to him, all they can see is the top of his green woolen cap sticking out of the neck of his tomato-red jacket.

"Worked at the rocket range for a time. Till they closed it down, then started putting my own business together where I could." Conrad bangs the tin plates and cutlery together as he washes.

Chuck wakes with a start.

"Rocket range?" This has grabbed Richard Rowan's interest. He had been singularly quiet until now.

"Ask Chuck about it," Conrad says. "We did a little tour of the abandoned buildings yesterday."

Richard Rowan regards Chuck with the inquisitive

look of a monkey inspecting an unfamiliar piece of fruit. But he says nothing.

Hal is also paying heed to Chuck. "Is this a place you want us to tape?"

"Yeah, maybe." Chuck seems to be turning something over in his mind. "Local color." He notices Conrad scrutinizing him. "Got a project I'm thinking on. The rocket range might work as a studio."

Hal tries not to look at Pete and Lucas, who are looking from Chuck to him with undisguised surprise.

"Nothing more than an idea, yet." Chuck directs this to his production crew.

A fleeting smile passes over Richard Rowan's face as he folds his long fingers around his mug of tepid tea.

Guy finishes his meal and takes his plate to the counter, where he nudges Conrad away from the dishpan. "Go sit down," he says, relieving his friend of the sopping dishcloth.

Conrad reaches into his backpack and retrieves a bottle of Rémy Martin. "That meal deserves a nightcap." He passes the bottle around.

The sound of Guy washing up is punctuated by the gurgle of brandy decanted into tea mugs. Listening to the umber bottle's progress around the room, Guy glances over his shoulder to see if Allsun is drinking. A shot of brandy would do her good, he thinks. It was his grandmother's cure-all. Brandy and mother's milk. Mother's milk! With the three of them together again, he has fallen back into the role of primary caregiver and chief bottle washer. Guy flings a wet mug out onto the counter and it skims recklessly on a film of water toward the edge. He catches it before it can crash to the floor. Allsun had said, when she returned with Conrad, that she didn't see the point of taking up a hospital bed. The doctor had given her and Neal oxygen when they arrived at the hospital, but had admitted to her that he could do nothing more than observe their condition. Well, as far as she was concerned, she didn't have a condition that some sleep wouldn't correct. And Guy knew from experience that Allsun could not, would not sleep in a hospital room. Not without chemical persuasion. Perhaps, if Neal's condition had not improved, if he hadn't stabilized, she would have at least stayed in Churchill.

Talk idles on, fueled by Conrad's burnt wine. The tower hut is becoming increasingly close, body heat taking over from the small heater. The gas lamp presides over the party with flickering interest.

It doesn't take long before yawns follow words, a signal to Guy it's time to assign bunks and shut the camp down for the night. It means moving the media bunch out into the cold, which should drive the alcohol out of their veins before they start down the ladder to the Tundra Buggy. Guy waits politely for a break in Pete and Lucas's banter.

"Pete being Canadian and all," Lucas says in his best patronizing voice, "thinks Americans are . . . what's that word you use, Pete?"

"Nescient, Lucas. Sounds like the static on your tapes." Pete grins at the soundman.

"Yeah, static, that's it. Pete gives us static because we know less about Canada than he does about America."

"Hell, I know more about the States than you and Hal put together. Ask me a question, anything, come on." Pete uses the two-handed come-and-get-me gesture, baiting both Lucas and Hal. It's obvious Pete has ridden this horse with no name across America many times. Hal is not going along.

"What's this thing you call 'the states'?" Lucas asks dryly.

"Anything below," Pete underscores *below*, "the 49th parallel that's not Latino. Despite names like New Mexico, California, Montana."

Laughter in the room turns Pete's droll, straight face into a broad grin.

Guy, taking advantage of the pause, taps the kettle hard with a knife. "A draw," he announces. "Sorry, fellows, we should be thinking about getting set up for the night."

"You wanna tuck us in?" Pete puts on a fake moue. "But we're having so much fun."

"Yeah, and I'm going to hold your hand on the way to the bathroom, too." Guy lets the sniggers pass before he gets down to business. "I'm not kidding. Rule number one around here ... no one sets foot on solid ground without an escort. The toilet's in the storage cage below the tower. I'll take whoever has to go ... one at a time ... while Jud and Conrad cover us from the platform. The most dangerous time around here is after dark. The bears tuck themselves in under the tower, Tundra Buggy, and trailer." Guy notices Chuck jerk his chin up off his chest to exchange looks with Hal.

A BALEFUL WIND blows Guy in the hut door. He looks frozen to the bone. "Wouldn't you know it. The wind picks up just when people have to unbutton and coax sphincters open. A piss takes forever."

Allsun, huddled in a sleeping bag on one of the bunks, gives him a tired smile that says she appreciates his effort to make light.

"You want tea? I'm going make some. Thaw me out." He takes only his gloves off as he busies himself at the counter. "We finally got things sorted out in the Tundra Buggy. Jud and Conrad are going to bunk down there just in case we got a sleepwalker or two. Should be fine ... they've got a piss bucket ... furnace seems to be okay ... Jud and I replaced the valve." He turns at Allsun's prevailing silence. "You okay?"

"Couldn't stay there."

"No."

"Too many nights in hospitals. It's nearly four years, you know."

"I know."

Allsun finally looks at Guy. "They want me to pull the plug."

"What?" Guy sits, forgetting the tea.

"Damon's family . . . they want to take him off life support."

"Al, I didn't ... when did this happen?"

"They came to me a couple of weeks ago . . . pretty much the whole Pythias tribe. *Enough, enough*—that's all Mama Sophronia can say . . . enough, enough for who? I'm the one there at the hospital day and night, I'm the one paying most of the bills; enough for who?"

"What does Damon's doctor say?" Guy is trying to find some middle ground while he imagines what her life must be like now.

"What doctors say. They gave up treating him a long time ago. Food and water isn't medicine." Allsun waves a pale hand at the specters crowding her. "You want the cant? 'Nutrition and hydration are moral obligations I can relieve them of.' Damon's more than an obligation."

"Yes, of course—"

"And now Neal! I can't remember ... did I do the right thing?"

"Did you ... yes, yes. I don't know how you did it. You saved—"

The whistle on the kettle blows. Startled over the edge, Allsun cries.

Guy grabs up the kettle and flicks off the burner. He goes to Allsun, sits on the bunk, puts an arm around her shoulder. "You'll do the right thing. I know you."

"It wasn't supposed to be like this. We had it all planned, remember?" Allsun uses her sleeve on her dripping nose.

"You mean E&E? We were pretty naïve." Guy fishes the tail end of a roll of toilet paper from his jacket pocket. He wraps off a length for her.

"That wouldn't have stopped the three of you. You'd have made E&E work. Just like now, you're making the bear safety program work."

Guy smiles at Allsun. "Right, coach. The company logo you designed would have been great on team jackets."

"You making fun of me?" From behind the bouquet of toilet paper, Allsun looks as if she's set to cry again.

"No, not you." He hugs her. "You believed in us even when it started to fall apart. When Jane died—"

"Neal would have come around eventually, but when Damon—"

"No, Allsun. Neal wouldn't have partnered with me.

E&E, a company called Ecology and Ethics . . . he would have laughed in my face. And now we're both like Jonah, trying to make things right from inside the whale."

"You both do good work. Work that makes a difference."

Guy studies Allsun, getting a glimpse of what keeps her going. A fleeting glimpse.

"Not all change comes from the outside." Allsun seems stricken when she says these words. "How can I know? How can anyone know?"

"Know?" Guy shifts at the change in her voice. He hears the agony and leans forward to look into her eyes.

"Know Damon's world. The world he's living in right now. Is he trapped in hell? Is he on a journey? He might be in a better place than we are."

"You're right, Allsun. You can't know. Maybe it's time you started thinking about this world, about yourself."

"What do you mean?" Allsun glares at Guy. "I thought you'd be on my side."

"I am on your side. Firmly on your side. But Damon might consider you to be trapped in hell."

"Damon's your friend."

"So are you. And you deserve a life." Guy raises a hand to stay Allsun's protest. "I'm not telling you what you should do. But remember, it's your life too." Her eyes suddenly seem haunted. The little room has gone from frigid to close. He removes his jacket, leaving it beside Allsun on the bunk. At the counter he strikes a new match to light the stove.

When Guy turns back to Allsun, two mugs in his hands, she is asleep where she sits. He puts the mugs down. She doesn't awaken when he lifts her feet onto the bunk, pulls the sleeping bag up around her shoulders, and folds his jacket under her head.

Retrieving one of the steaming mugs of tea, he sits in the only chair the hut has to offer. Somehow the hard seat and stiff back feel good—solid, upright, functional. Simple traits in simple objects. What he would give to simplify the circus his life has become. But the older he gets, the more complex and confounding life is. Who were those people Allsun was talking about? Could he possibly have had the audacity to call a consulting company Ecology and Ethics? Now, in his implacable government position, he'd get a big laugh out of a company with such a name offering its services. How did he manage to become a cynic, while Allsun in all her grief has remained trusting?

Guy studies Allsun's face. He sees the changes—pinched lines between her brows, the cheekbones high and hollow. There's a Joni Mitchell cast to her, the pale, dry look of someone driven. It's not the drive so much—he's driven by his profession, his job—it's the total abandonment of self to the work. Perhaps if he and Neal were running their own environmental company, he too would have eyes perpetually turned inward to the task of making it all work. But to what end? Why do people do the jobs they do? What do they hope to accomplish in this world?

Allsun stirs, and strands of her long red hair fall across her face. Guy notices for the first time how the deep red is faded and frayed. Neal had told him about her regular routine of staying with Damon until midnight, then going home to work in her darkroom the rest of the night. He wonders if she's rubbing fingers wet with chemicals through her hair the way he read some famous photographer had, bleaching the color out of his hair, turning it a lizard green. What does she see in those fixed pools of chemicals? Transformation, perhaps?

Allsun hadn't set out to be a photojournalist. In the beginning it had been a way to support herself and Damon's special care needs. Guy hoped it was more than just a job for her.

What about the others out here, snoring blissfully in the Tundra Buggy? Someone like Conrad loves what he does. Chuck Ford's nature show: does he think it makes a difference? And his young assistant, Jud, what's he doing out at the Cape—earning credits, gaining experience toward what purpose? Jud had been hired for him, not by him, and Guy had heard through the grapevine that strings were pulled in what should have been a position filled on merit. Apparently Jud's father has some connections, the nature of the network had not been passed along with the gossip.

Staring into his empty cup, he thinks, *Avoir le trou de cul en* [illegible] *bras*. He says aloud to the walls, "If my ass is under my arm, I better haul it off to bed. Big day tomorrow."

Below on the tower platform, Chuck Ford and Jud Ash are having a smoke. Jud is reminded of how much he hates the burn in his lungs that comes with an occasional cigarette.

"So you're one of mine," Chuck says. "Wouldn't know you to see you. But I don't get up to Oregon much.

Good bunch of men, they run the show pretty much on their own."

Jud bristles at Chuck's sense of ownership, although he suspects Chuck has offered it as a compliment. "I'm not in Oregon anymore. At university in Vancouver."

"That's right, I remember now. You're our Canadian recruiter. Well, good to meet y'all." Chuck offers his hand as if they were in fact meeting for the first time. "Should have recognized you as one of mine; you got attitude."

Jud takes Chuck's outstretched hand and looks him in the eye. "So, tell me about the LIB project you got planned for up here."

Chuck takes the younger man's measure. "Ford Productions . . . looking for a studio."

"What's up here for a production company? More polar bear pictures?" Jud mixes skepticism with sarcasm —more attitude.

"You gotta admit they're magical, sell themselves. Can't run LIB without money, big money for an organization that size. It's how I've always done it . . . Ford Productions supports LIB." Chuck tosses his cigarette butt over the rail, down onto the tundra.

Jud smiles, knowing Guy will see it tomorrow morning and have a fit. "Yeah, I know the story. But I also know that where you go, LIB goes. You want my best guess . . . you're up here because of GRAND. Bourassa's been spouting off about his Great Replenishment and Northern Development Canal again. He's talking about putting a dam in at Moosonee to keep the rivers from flowing into James Bay. it's not hard to put two and two together, it's not rocket science." He smirks in the dark at his little joke.

"No doubt about it, there's lots to be concerned about up here ... mining, oil and gas exploitation in the high Arctic. Yeah, lots to be worried about if you love the old girl. Just look at where we're standing. Sky like that ... love to see those northern lights." Chuck puts a match to another cigarette. Offers it to Jud.

Jud notices how Chuck's hand shakes. Either he's freezing his butt off singing the praises of Mother Nature or he needs a drink. "You changing the subject?" Jud passes on the smoke.

"What subject?" Chuck bounces onto the balls of his feet, which gives him some height and the plywood platform an alarming wow. "Look down there. See the bears. I knew it. Shit, they're crawling in under that trailer."

"Yeah, they sleep under there a lot. Got a researcher that way. That's why the door's boarded up." Jud tosses this out. He wants to keep Chuck talking despite the cold. Eventually he'll get what he wants from this little man.

"Killed?" Chuck watches, mesmerized, as a thousand-pound bear ambles by below them. His rump sports a number ten as if he's a contestant in some all night dance-a-thon. He's cruising for a partner.

"Yeah. Right there." Jud points to a place in front of the trailer. The ambling bear casts a night shadow over the ground at which they stare. "She came out the door and down a ramp that used to be there. On her way to the storage cage. Never made it. Bear came out from under the trailer. They're big, but they're fast. One swipe ... took her head off before Guy had a chance to shoot and kill it."

"Guy? The one running this show?" Chuck's examining

Jud out of the corner of his eye as he keeps the polar bear in sight.

"Yeah. And that's not all. Neal, the one in hospital at Churchill, he was out here too. Him and her had a thing going. I heard he freaked for awhile."

Chuck gives Jud a look that questions how it is he's so well informed. "When did this happen?"

"I don't know. Maybe five years ago. Something like that. They were graduate students. The woman, I don't remember her name, was their doctoral supervisor." Jud seems disengaged. In reality, he's trying to figure out how to keep Chuck talking, now that the second cigarette is done.

Chuck turns toward the gangplank that will take him over to the grudging warmth of the Tundra Buggy. "You going to turn your headlamp on and check around under that ramp?"

"Sure. I can do that." Jud switches on the lamp and checks under the platform by training the beam of light on the gaps between the sheets of plywood. Convinced that he can go to the edge of the platform without having a bear rise up from below, he scans under the lumber of the gangplank. "Do you know this photographer, Richard Rowan?" Jud asks from his circle of light.

"Never met him before today. Why? You know him?" Chuck comes up cautiously behind Jud.

"No. But it looked to me like he had a lot to say to you." Jud is kneeling, directing his head from side to side so the beam from his headlamp sweeps the ground. "I got the impression he knew some things he shouldn't."

Chuck contemplates the back of Jud's head. He remains silent.

Jud turns to Chuck, suddenly aware of how close the other man is. He stands, all in one fluid motion. He floods Chuck's face with light.

"Fuck. Get that thing outta my face." Chuck shields his eyes.

Jud reaches up and clicks the light off. He faces Chuck in the dark.

"You're right, Rowan knows a lot of things he shouldn't about me and about LIB. I don't know how he knows, but I'm going to find out. Then I'll do something about him." Chuck has stepped close enough to be staring Jud in the eyes.

Jud recognizes what he sees in Chuck's eyes. He knows hate when he sees it.

CAPE CHURCHILL
October 31, 1986

THE LAUNCHING PAD VIBRATES with tension. Chuck is looking through the lens of Pete's camera. "No, shit no, this won't work." Chuck jerks away from the camera with such force that it wobbles on the tripod. Pete puts a hand out to steady his prized piece of equipment. "We're not shooting from here. That's all there is to it." Chuck turns on Guy, who is coming down the ladder from the tower hut. "Gotta find us another spot. This is the shits."

Guy regards Chuck with a calmness that belies his desire to deck him. From the get-go this morning, Ford has been a pain in the ass. Either he didn't sleep well or he's got a burr up his bum; Guy couldn't care less. He just wants this man out of his camp. Get the footage or tape or whatever the hell they call it and leave him to do his work. Time is running out on the research program and he has to waste valuable energy on a prick like this. Mustering up a civil tone, Guy says, "What about the trailer roof?"

Chuck looks over. "Still not low enough. How we going to get decent shots that high off the ground?"

Jud arrives on the launching pad, the Winchester slung over his shoulder. They knew he was coming before he placed a foot on the first rung of the ladder. The rank odor of seal and Ten Dead Horses heralded his approach. "Sandwich is made," he says.

Pete holds his nose and speaks. His voice sounds as if it's coming through a kazoo. "Remind me not to stand next to you. You're bear bait."

"So, what are you going to do about this?" Chuck demands of Guy.

Jud, who, while he worked in the storage cage, had been listening to Chuck carp, steps in with a suggestion. "How about the top of the storage cage?"

"Not safe," is Guy's immediate response. "Within reach. You've seen bears stand up against the cage."

"Yeah, thought we could lay tarps along the edge. Make a visual barrier. As long as Pete and Lucas stayed dead center." Jud glances at Pete. "Otherwise, the bears will treat it like a cookie jar."

Chuck eyeballs the storage cage at the foot of the tower. It would put the camera about eight feet off the ground. "Yeah, might work," he says, as if it's his decision to make.

Guy studies his assistant, trying to decide whether he can trust Jud's plan. "Means moving the observation cage." Guy points to where the observation cage sits near the bear barbecue. "Can't see the bait site from the storage cage. Lab trailer's in the way."

"We could put the tarps up and let the bears inspect them," Jud offers as a compromise. "See how it goes."

Guy shakes his head. "And Chuck, you still want to be positioned inside the observation cage?"

"Yeah, absolutely."

Guy looks him over. "This is more trouble than it's worth."

"Not to me." Chuck is quick to protect his interests.

"No, I don't expect so, but this is a research camp, after all. There's work to be done here." Guy is only too aware of ice forming on the Bay. Twenty-four to forty-eight hours and the bears could be gone. In less time than it takes to deal with the likes of Chuck Ford, the Cape polar bears could put enough distance between them and the camp to put the kibosh on this year's program.

"Tell you what." Chuck sounds half-way conciliatory. "Hal and me, we'll help move the cage. Pete and Lucas can give you a hand with the tarps. Get this show on the road and get out of your hair. How's that?"

"Okay. Here's how it works." Guy makes sure he has everyone's undivided attention. "Jud, you take the Winchester and the Riot Gun. Put some gas in the ATV, you'll need it to pull the cage over. Take a couple of crowbars. The base of the observation cage is frozen into the gravel. I'll ride shotgun while we tarp the storage cage. And Conrad will be up here on the platform with the deterrent arsenal and his rifle." Guy looks to each man individually for confirmation. "Alright, keep your eyes open."

It doesn't take long for Guy and the others to roll the fiberglass tarps into fat orange sausages that they secure with bungee cords to the outer edges of the storage cage's mesh roof. The eight-foot-high steel cage now looks like a ten-foot-high cabana, northern style.

Pete and Lucas retreat to the shelter of the Tundra

Buggy. Their thin southern blood doesn't keep their feet and hands warm for long.

Guy climbs up to where Conrad is posted on the launching pad. He wants to know if Conrad is free to fly a survey down to the Owl River maternity dens. Perhaps tomorrow, if he can get rid of Chuck.

As they talk, Guy watches the other men working around the base of the observation cage. "Shit, look at that! Think they'd never had a crowbar in their hands before ... hitting the cage more often than the damn ground."

"Sounds like you've had your hands full out here." Conrad keeps his eyes on the surrounding terrain.

"The last couple of days have been a bitch. We're pretty far behind. That's why I want to get in there and get what data we can from Owl River." Guy observes Jud as he loops a chain through the slats of the observation cage and attaches the free end to the hitch on the ATV with its half-eaten seat. The vinyl upholstery is a polar bear delicacy.

"Too bad about the accident. Can't say I've known many of those propane heaters to leak like that." Conrad glances at Guy.

"Allsun saved the day, that's for sure. But I don't think she should be out here ... she looks like hell. I'm going to see if I can talk her into going back to Churchill with you. Get checked out at the clinic, at least. She won't go back into the hospital, I know that," Guy reflects with more agitation than the topic warrants. He doesn't like the way the observation cage is bumping across the gravel behind the ATV. Jud has chained it so that, instead of gliding sled-like, it's bouncing from corner to corner. "Merde," Guy mutters.

"She got something against hospitals?" Conrad would like to know more about this woman, who doesn't look like she has a frail bone in her body.

"What?" Guy is preoccupied with the fate of thousands of dollars' worth of custom steelwork rebounding off frozen rocks. "Oh, Allsun? Spends most days in one."

"How come?" Conrad frowns down on the pothole lake with its esker of Ungava willow. "Thought she was a photographer."

"Her husband's ..." Guy is trying to decide whether to signal Jud to stop and get him to reposition the chain, "in a coma."

"Oh, I see."

Guy directs his attention to Conrad, hearing something in his friend's voice. "Been that way for awhile now. She's out here 'cause she's got a decision to make."

Conrad turns his scrutiny from the land to Guy. For an instant their eyes meet, then Conrad looks off to the Bay in the distance with its parade of restless bears.

Guy is left to get his head around a new idea: there might be someone else for Allsun. Not that she stopped attracting men when she married; it's just that since he's known her, she's always been completely wrapped up in Damon. On some level, Guy assumed that one of them would take care of her when Damon died. He knows Neal has feelings for Allsun that he has not openly acknowledged. Guy suspects these feelings are at least part of the reason Neal talked her into coming to the Cape. But there is no doubt in Guy's mind that Allsun was meant to be a buffer between himself and Neal, between Neal and Jane's ghost. This he considers selfish of Neal.

A shout comes from behind Guy and Conrad. "Can I join you?" Richard Rowan in standing on the Tundra Buggy deck.

"Let me check." Guy bends down and peers through the chinks in the plywood platform, then surveys under the gangway. "It's okay," he calls back.

All the while, Richard Rowan had been clicking off shots of Guy and Conrad. Once across, he switches to the other Nikon around his neck and kneels to photograph the deterrence guns. Finished, he says to Guy, "Pete and Lucas were telling me about this observation cage. Any chance of me shooting from in there?"

"Depends on Chuck. Have to talk to him." Guy points to where Chuck, Hal and Jud are struggling to right the observation cage at a photographically prescribed distance from the storage cage. "Looks like they could use some help."

Rowan tucks his cameras inside his jacket and heads for the ladder. Guy does a second sweep, looking for bears hiding under the Tundra Buggy to one side of the tower and the lab trailer to the other—back and forth like a minesweeper searching for deadly bundles. As Rowan swings down the ladder, Allsun arrives on the platform from the tower hut. "You should've got me up," she tells Guy.

"Hey, Sleeping Beauty," he says.

"Yeah, right. Is there water in the Tundra Buggy so I can wash? None in the hut." Allsun's face is barely visible with her toque pulled down low and her parka hood up.

"Morning," Conrad says over his shoulder. "You feeling better?"

"Better than I look."

Conrad chuckles, giving her a fleeting glance.

"I'll check it out," Guy offers.

"I'm not an invalid." She moves toward the gangplank, then turns back to Guy and slugs him in the arm with her fist. "Sorry."

"Coming across anyway to put a pot of tea on. We're going need to warm up before we get things rolling." Guy takes one last look at the observation cage as the men hump it into place. He yells down to Jud, "I'll get you some water to freeze the base to the ground."

Nothing but waste water in the Tundra Buggy. A lot of waste water. Guy will have to remind his guests this isn't a damned hotel. He's carrying the axe and a five-gallon jerry can, the Winchester slung over his shoulder. Allsun walks out to the pothole lake beside him with another of the red plastic containers. "One can would have been enough for now," he says to her.

"I'm okay, Guy. Stop worrying about me."

They walk in silence, alert to their vulnerability. Guy trots backwards a few paces so he can scan the open tundra behind them.

"Give me the axe to carry," Allsun demands. "Free up a hand."

Guy is about to decline, then thinks better of it.

They don't waste any time getting to the lake. Once there, it seems to take forever to get through the ice and fill the cans.

Allsun stands guard. The light is flat, making it hard to distinguish shadow from snow from bear. She's tense and made even more so by having to keep not only her gloves but also her mitts on while she holds what has become a super-cold piece of metal. She's thankful it's a pump action shotgun, not a rifle. The shotgun is better suited to these conditions.

"The ice is thicker than it was the last time I was out here," Guy remarks as he chops a hole with the axe. "The storm, these deep-freeze temperatures ... the bears could be gone tomorrow."

Allsun glances down at where he works. "It's going to have to be bigger, isn't it?"

"Not much." Guy hacks around the edges of the opening he has made.

"The can won't fit through," Allsun observes, impatient.

Guy scans the area. Gives her a look of concern. He pulls a small pot with a handle out of his backpack. "We bail." With a flourish, he waves the pot at Allsun.

"Wouldn't it be easier to chop a bigger hole and stick the jerry cans under water?" Allsun asks.

Guy is bailing rapidly, a practiced hand. "No, while the can's filling, the ice just floats back in and covers the hole."

Allsun turns slowly, hunting the landscape, the Winchester in a two-handed grip. She is monitoring a land with few hiding places, but she is more nervous than Guy would expect her to be. Allsun, the cool one in a crisis; he realizes the strain of her life is taking its toll.

On the way back they are followed. A gang of three juveniles comes out of the low willows. Polar bears two and three years old are perhaps the most dangerous. About half the height and weight of an adult, it's not size but boldness that makes them so. At the Cape, cubs are weaned early, their mothers driving them off at around eighteen months. Not yet skilled hunters, young bears are hungrier than the adults, at least the adult males.

Guy assesses the bears shadowing them; they are as big as the mature black bear that tried to join him and Neal one morning in their two-man tent. That was a Banff National Park bear, habituated to people and just as dangerous as these barren-land predators.

The gang may not be fully-fledged hunters, but they're tundra smart. Guy and Allsun both recognize the strategy the bears have put into action. One young bear falls in behind Allsun and Guy, while the others move ahead, cutting off their retreat to the camp.

The Winchester, a short-barreled 12-gauge, is loaded with a three-slug system: two plastic Ferret slugs, and a lead slug. Ferret slugs are most effective at twenty-seven yards. If the two lead bears hold their trajectory, Guy will be within optimum range when he reaches the 175m or 191yd test marker staked at the periphery of the study site.

There is no way Allsun and Guy can outrun their stalkers. It's known that grizzly bears are sixty-six percent faster than the fastest human. These young bears could outdistance a car doing 20 mph in a playground zone. And this is their playground.

Guy passes the test marker, followed by Allsun, who is trotting backwards, checking on the lone hunter in the rear.

Dropping the jerry can, Guy raises the shotgun to his shoulder. He fires on the advance party, one bear then the other. The first is hit in the rump with a ferret slug and veers away, turning to look at its hind leg. Guy misses the second bear. It had altered its stride instantly in response to the first hit on its companion. He has a kill load left in the Winchester.

Out of the pocket of his parka Guy produces a flare

pencil and a fistful of plastic-encased emergency flare cartridges. Mitts off, he slides a cartridge down the barrel of the spring-loaded shooter. Holding it away from himself with a straight arm, Guy fires at the bears. An explosion of red light lands between the two bears. Both bears back away a few paces to reassess but do not retreat.

With his hand already in his other pocket, Guy thrusts the flare pencil and cartridges at Allsun. "Keep 'em busy while I reload."

Launched from the tower, a Rocket Banger spirals orange against the gray sky and explodes—thunder after lightning—above the bears.

Guy turns on the bear behind them, hitting it in the shoulder with a Ferret slug. Swiveling like a turret gunner, he fires on the other two. A rump hit. Guy now has two dancing bears. It's enough. The bears retreat for good this time. A safe distance away they regroup, stopping to take in the camp.

Guy and Allsun retrieve the jerry cans and pass the remaining test zone markers like athletes in a modified biathlon.

They are within striking distance of the Tundra Buggy. Allsun trips and the jerry can skids across the icy rocks and snow. She's on her knees, breathing hard, her hands shaking where they hang against her thighs.

Throwing the other jerry can like a curling rock down the ice toward the Tundra Buggy, Guy helps Allsun to her feet. He kicks her jerry can along in front of them as he walks her to the Tundra Buggy deck.

Guy releases the stairs that are stored up under the Buggy deck, then climbs up and opens the solid wooden gate to the observation deck. Stowing the shotgun, he comes back to help her up. Gently Guy leads Allsun to a bunk and goes outside for the jerry cans of hard-won water.

He locks the deck gate and bends to the trap door in the deck floor. As he hauls the stairs up under the carriage by a chain, he vows to be firm. She's going back into Churchill.

When Guy returns, Allsun is asleep in a fetal curl, her spine a question mark. He covers her with a sleeping bag.

THE BARBECUE IS smoking, the stench of rancid seal meat and Ten Dead Horses billowing over the camp. They wait, crammed into the tower hut. Guy is hosting a tea party upstairs so Allsun in wonderland can sleep undisturbed in the Tundra Buggy.

There will be time for one brew, Guy predicts. He has just managed to get the tea into the cups when Conrad signals him to the window. Guy takes the binoculars. To the naked eye it would appear as if snowdrifts on the horizon are undulating, a trick of the slanting northern light. Instead, it is an exodus of ice bears led inland to the camp by their noses.

"Party's over. We better get down there," Guy announces to the room.

CHUCK GETS HIS crew set up on top of the storage cage, and then he and Hal retreat inside it. Conrad is riding shotgun from the deck of the Tundra Buggy, while Jud is doing the same from the top of the lab trailer. Guy has the deterrence arsenal and his clipboard laid out on the launching pad. Richard Rowan swings down from the tower ladder beside Guy. "Should I head for the cage?" he asks.

"The cage?" Guy thought everything had been arranged. Rowan was to shoot from the platform, not one of the cages.

"The observation cage."

"I thought Chuck was—"

"He offered me the first go."

"Sure, fine." Guy looks for Chuck and sees him in the storage cage. "Go ahead. I'll watch out for you."

Richard Rowan shuts himself inside a steel box barely big enough to contain him. He crouches, stamps his feet, hugs himself and his cameras, stashed out of the cold inside his jacket. Then he goes down on one knee like an Inuk hunter.

There are now five polar bears in camp, all adult males, the dominant population at the Cape. They are inspecting the grounds: buggy wheels, lab trailer, fuel drums and, ultimately, subject to hierarchy, the two cages with their tantalizing smells of seal meat and humans. Much of what is taking place at the foot of the tower has to do more with bear politics and less with camp reconnaissance.

Allsun appears beside Guy on the platform with her cameras. Guy gives her a questioning look.

"You shouldn't let me sleep on the job, Guy. What kind of camp manager are you, anyway?" She gives him what might pass as a smile if he didn't know better. "What's happening?"

"I'm waiting for a few of the bears to reach the bait site. I want to measure the difference in deterrence time between the bears randomly exploring the camp and those whose focus is the bait." Guy makes sure they stay elbow to elbow at the center of the platform—the only place they are out of reach of bears who could easily stand eleven feet tall on their hind legs.

"Why?"

"Give that lot a chance to film, for one thing. But I want to know whether the camp bears are more easily deterred. This is important information in terms of the configuration of existing and future industrial camps in the north. The question being, where and how best to store food in relationship to camp quarters and daily activity."

"Oh, is that all?"

"Don't take the piss out of me. You asked."

Allsun scrutinizes the bait site, then checks below to see what shots are available. As she raises the Nikon to her eye, a white snout appears from between the tower legs, coming from directly below the platform. With explosive speed the bear leaps, ripping a tarp from its place along the top edge of the storage cage. Pete's camera on its tripod starts to tip. Pete goes with it, reaching, bending to bring the camera and himself back to center.

The bear makes another leap. A powerful paw swipes Pete's shoulder. Lucas grabs Pete by the hood of his jacket. The bear falls back to the ground without its quarry as Lucas does some fancy footwork to stabilize himself and Pete. Tenaciously, Pete has hung onto the camera.

The stunned silence is broken by a pop from the Tundra Buggy deck. Conrad has launched a Ferret slug. Hit, the bear bolts to the side, only to make another lightning-fast leap for the top of the storage cage. It captures the dangling tarp, rips it away completely and drags it out [illegible] trailer.

"Pete!" Guy shouts across, "do you and Lucas wanna come down?"

"No thanks," Pete shouts back.

"Is it safe?" [illegible] bellows from inside the cage.

Laughter. They're all laughing, tension released in puffs of white breath like air from so many chaffed-red balloons.

"Stick close," Guy advises. "Lucas, watch Pete, keep him centered."

"As safe as downtown Washington in the dead of night," Richard Rowan's comment floats above the observation cage like dialogue above a comic strip scene.

Guy focuses on his data sheet, recording the numbers on the backs of two bears ambling toward the bait site. He clocks the rate of their approach. Glancing around, he does a quick check on the whereabouts of the other three bears. One is behind the lab trailer dining on orange fiberglass and plastic. The two remaining bears are circling Richard Rowan, photographing from inside the observation cage.

Rowan keeps up a running dialogue with his subjects as he pivots and shoots. The bears seem superior in their silence. The man in the cage is not their immediate concern. Establishing ownership is. The larger of the two bears huffs at its rival then snaps its jaws. Swaying its lowered head from side to side, ears back, the aggressor stands sideways to its opponent. When the rival does not give quarter, the instigator charges, head low, mouth wide open. A hissing roar of sharply expelled breath clouds the air between them. The rival backs up. Head lowered, the attacker charges again, biting its adversary on the neck and pounding its shoulder with a front paw. Without warning, the two bears rise on their hind legs and come together like sumo wrestlers. With more grace than their human counterparts would exhibit, they grapple and push, each attempting to topple and pin the other to the ground. The rival falls, swinging and biting. Mouths wide open, teeth bared, they lock jaws briefly, then part. The fallen bear rises and backs from the ring. Neither has drawn blood, neither has lost face.

The winner puts his muzzle against the bars of the cage and calmly examines the man. Eyes of black agate penetrate with a gaze so hypnotic it surely must hold hunters spellbound. The gaze prevails as a paw is slid through the bars. Claws as dark and polished as the eyes stretch toward the prize. Richard Rowan backs away. The paw is withdrawn.

Suddenly the bear rears up, slamming the cage with all the force of its massive front legs. Again and again the bear bullies the cage, causing it to rock with the impact.

Rowan is crouched, shooting up into the face of the bear.

On all fours, the bear rams the cage, putting a shoulder to the door. As it backs away for another attempt, the door swings out. Open.

In a split second Richard Rowan pulls the door shut, but not before the bear notices there is an opening.

Guy grabs up the riot gun, shoulders and shoots, firing almost simultaneously with Conrad and Jud. The bear is hit with a barrage of Ferret slugs and a rubber bullet.

It takes two steps back and shakes itself as if to dislodge pests.

"Richard, latch the door," Guy shouts.

Rowan fumbles at the cage door. "It's broken." His words are slivers of ice.

"Keep him off the cage!" Guy shouts to the others with guns.

Still, the polar bear advances on the cage. It pushes the door with a paw and raises its head to snap at Rowan's fingers, which are holding the door shut.

Head raised, the bear's shoulder is revealed. Guy sees his target. A shot. The bear slumps against the cage door. Another shot, like a current of electricity along the massive body. The bear does not rise to it.

Guy lowers the Winchester and wipes his face with his glove. Allsun sees the tears freeze on his cheeks.

Richard Rowan falls against the back wall of the cage and slides down onto his heels. He rocks.

Conrad breaks the unnatural silence. He shouts to Guy, "Better clear the camp."

Jud takes aim at the bear below his position on top of the lab trailer. A Ferret slug at such close range has the tarp-chewing bear on the run.

The bears fighting over the bait sandwich are not so easily displaced. Conrad makes a dash for the helicopter. He doesn't have to take the chopper into the air. The thunder of the powered up rotors is enough to drive the bears off.

Conrad cuts the engines. As the din dies down, Allsun hears Chuck shout up to Pete, above him on the storage cage roof, "Did you get it? All of it? Holy shit! We got lucky . . ."

Allsun puts her hand on Guy's arm. He starts as if from a trance. "I'm sorry," she says.

Guy stares down at the bear. It holds Richard Rowan captive by the weight of its presence.

Conrad is beside them on the platform. "I'll get the others to help me move the bear," he says to Guy in a voice that is barely a whisper.

Guy has not taken his eyes from the dead polar bear. "I'll do it." He raises his head and shouts to Jud, "We're going to ground."

It's all Guy, Conrad and Allsun can do to roll the dead weight of the bear away from the cage door. Chuck and Hal are more than willing to help, but Guy makes them stay in the storage cage.

Richard Rowan is released. Then too are the others, who are now aware of how cold they are. On the way to the tower, Chuck turns to Guy. "I'd like the hide. I'll pay for it."

Guy ignores Chuck. As they hustle to the tower ladder, Conrad explains to Chuck that it's against the law to keep or sell any part of a defense-killed bear.

BY THE TIME Guy and Jud are finished collecting data on the dead bear, the heater in the tower hut is lit, its warmth eating up the condensation of breath and damp clothing. The fug is redolent with alcohol fumes. Pete holds his jacket in one hand and a glass in the other. Both hands shake as he examines the tear in the slick fabric.

Richard Rowan's face is flushed. It looks as if he's had a few pulls of Wild Turkey with brandy chasers. "Nothing like ripstop nylon," he says to Pete. "The bear would have had a better chance with Lucas's leather jacket." Everyone glances at Lucas's fleece-lined aviator jacket, a well-worn signature piece. Richard has succeeded in drawing attention away from himself. He's trying to put together his own version of what happened to him in the cage.

Pete and Lucas make eye contact, and big grins form on their faces. They look like two boys saved from disaster. Richard's observation acts as a reminder—they have shared an adventure, they'll have a story to tell.

Chuck has been waiting for Guy's return. "So, what'll you do with the carcass?" He hasn't given up on his desire for a souvenir.

Guy believes Chuck is asking about the data they have just collected. "Standard retrieval . . . a tooth, blood sample, measurements for weight, height, length . . . that kind of thing."

"A tooth, you say. Wouldn't mind one of those." Chuck is the type who asks for what he wants.

Guy stares into Chuck's face. "This ain't no fucking amusement park." He's about to say more when the radio cracks the fragile shell of a sudden silence. Guy swings around and reaches for the microphone. He thumbs the talk switch. "Thorpe here, go ahead."

"Dr. Thomas, Churchill Hospital. Your colleague, Neal Casimir, will be released tomorrow, at his own insistence. He's requesting someone pick him up and fly him out to the Cape. Can you arrange?"

"Yes, I can do that." Guy's brow shows his concern. "How is he?" His question is tentative.

"Not as well as he thinks," Dr. Thomas is perturbed. "But I'm just the doctor, what do I know."

"Thanks, Dr. Thomas. There'll be someone there to talk to him tomorrow." Guy nods at Allsun.

"Got it. I'm clear." The doctor's voice is replaced by static.

Guy flicks the switch and hangs up the microphone. He turns to Conrad.

"Any time," Conrad says.

"Allsun?" Guy asks.

"Yeah, I'll check up on him."

Guy pulls Conrad and Allsun together near the door. They close ranks and the others in the room create privacy by creating conversation.

Guy puts his arm around Allsun's shoulder. "I want you to see Dr. Thomas."

"Of course," Allsun says. "I'll talk to him about Neal."

"I want you to let Dr. Thomas check you out. You're not as well as you think you are either." Guy holds her gaze.

"So this isn't about Neal?" she huffs.

"It's about both of you. I'm trusting you, Al, to listen to the doctor and do the right thing . . . for you and for him. I need to know you two will be okay. Do you understand?" Guy has never been more fragile, and Allsun senses his state. She doesn't want to burden him with any more worry.

"Alright. I'll take care of us." She smiles reassurance.

Relief floods his face. It lasts for only a moment, then Guy turns his attention to Conrad. "I'm going to take the dead bear out to the edge of the Bay. The other bears will make short work of it. That way it won't be a total waste," he says through clenched teeth. "Will you give me an escort in the chopper?"

"Yeah, sure. Of course." Conrad lays a hand on his friend's back. "I can take Allsun up with me and when you're done we can fly directly into Churchill. How's that sound?"

"Good. Really good."

They are joined by Richard Rowan, who had sat quietly while the others had reviewed, relived, retold the events of the day. To Conrad, Rowan says, "I'd like to go into Churchill."

Behind him Jud shoots Chuck a look. Their eyes meet for a split second, then move away seemingly absorbed in the production crew's wild storytelling.

GUY AND CONRAD cinch the chain across the great bear's chest as it lies on its back. It looks truly human now with the life gone out of its limbs: forelegs sprawled away from the chest like arms; hind legs relaxed apart, akimbo from the pelvis. The reclining posture of the polar bear has not been wasted on the native people of the north—a skinned bear is human-like in its musculature. They know a brother when they see one. The bones of the bear are more revered than the bones of ancestors. Guy thinks this and mourns.

As he hooks the chain to the ATV, Guy thanks Conrad and gives Allsun the thumbs up. She stows Conrad's rifle in the chopper's rear compartment and joins Richard Rowan in the bubble.

From the launching pad Jud and Chuck watch the preparations. The Jet Ranger lifts off and the two men on the tower platform wave, convinced they've seen the last of Richard Rowan.

The strange procession makes its way toward the bayshore with its sea ice. Guy sits as straight as if he were paddling a boat, not riding a three-wheeled vehicle across rough terrain that makes him wincingly aware of every rock the dead bear slides over. He could be Charon crossing the river Styx, accompanied by a flying harbinger. Guy does not know of Charon. And the wings of his bird whip wind into his streaming eyes.

CONRAD SETS DOWN at the Churchill airport. He has a small office in a hangar. It's cramped but tidy—a place for everything, everything in its place. The office suggests an organized mind, reassuring in a pilot.

He pulls out the chair from his metal desk and offers it and his telephone to Richard Rowan.

"Thanks, Conrad. I'll pay you for the long distance charges." He's dialing before Conrad can reply.

"Think I'll raid that vending machine down the hall." Allsun pats down her pockets for change. "I need a chocolate fix."

Conrad hands her a cookie tin.

"No thanks," she tells him. "This requires serious endorphin-producing chemicals in bar form."

Conrad shakes the container and it rattles like her dad's Player's tobacco tin full of nails, screws and tacks. "Change," he says. "Help yourself." Conrad hands it over. "I'll go warm up the truck."

Allsun finds the machine already dispensing to someone who looks as desperate as she feels. As she comes closer, she realizes he's more of a fiend than she is; he's filling a plastic shopping bag.

"That's a hell of a habit," Allsun comments, as she rattles the cookie tin.

"It's not for me," he says, without missing a beat, like someone feeding the slots in Vegas. "I forgot to buy Hallowe'en candy and my wife says the Super Market's run out. I'm S.O.L. if I come home empty-handed."

"So you're emptying the machine?" Either the hiss in her voice or the menacing rattle of the cookie tin gets his attention.

"Pretty much." He's looking at Allsun now. "What do you need?"

"A couple of boxes of M&M's, a couple of Aero bars." Allsun pries the lid off the tin. The rim is like a curved blade beneath her fingernails. It reminds her of her grandmother's innovative and treacherous cookie tins: discarded movie reel canisters from the '40s. Two flat metal disks the size of twin pizza pans, whose thin edges fit together with diabolical precision. Tamper proof.

The Candy Man fishes around in his shopping bag like some oversized trick or treater. "Candy-coated peanuts?" he asks.

"No, the chocolate ones." The only real cure for stress.

Pointing to the vending machine, he says, "They're still in there. Stuck." He looks her over. "You wanna help me tip it? Shake'em loose?"

Allsun sizes up the situation, the fat-bellied machine. "Sure."

They're wrestling the Metal Bandit like a tag team when Conrad intervenes with a sharp, two-fingers in the mouth whistle—a referee without stripes. "What is this, a mugging?"

"More like the WWF," Allsun says. "And he's the bad

guy." She shoulders the vending machine. It spits out two packages of M&M's.

"Is this what you were after?" Conrad retrieves the brown boxes from the chute.

"Yeah." Allsun takes change from the cookie tin and pays her hit-man partner. "I'll put this back in your office." She rattles the tin at Conrad.

"That's quite the stash, Bill," Conrad says to The Candy Man. "You catering a flight to Winnipeg?" He chuckles.

Bill is plying the machine with silver again, his concentration fixed.

Since Bill seems reluctant to break his rhythm, Allsun answers for him. "Tonight's Hallowe'en. Hadn't crossed my mind ... or his."

"Oh, yeah." Conrad draws this out as it dawns on him. "You're in for a treat, Allsun." Conrad shakes his head in agreement with his own thoughts.

"Trick or treat." Allsun offers him one of the Aero bars he paid for, as they walk down the hall to his office.

They approach the closed door. The sound of Richard's voice stops them outside the office.

"I'll drop Richard at the hotel, then I'll take you over to the hospital," Conrad offers.

Allsun is popping M&M's into her mouth at a rate that would put a two-fisted child to shame. "Maybe we could do a quick tour of Churchill and I could get some shots. I've still got an assignment to think about."

"Can do. What about a few local bear stories, could you use some of those?" Conrad notices that Richard has lowered his voice on the other side of the door.

"Yeah, maybe. Can't hurt." Allsun crumples the candy box in her fist.

"Let's go back and have a little chat with Bill." Conrad nods at the door. "Sounds like Richard's still tied up."

They walk back down the hall. "Bill," Conrad says, "this is Allsun Skelly."

The man now formally known as Bill looks as if they just woke him.

Conrad continues, "She's doing a story for *Up Here*. I'm introducing her to the Polar Bear Capital of the World." He pauses to see if Bill has caught up. "Thought you should tell her your story." Conrad turns to Allsun. "Bill's ground crew here at the airport."

"Sure," Bill says. "I'll just finish this roll of quarters. That's all the little beggars are getting out of me. It's cost a small fortune."

"You'll be a hit, though," Allsun observes. "This is premium loot. Beats suckers and candy kisses all to hell."

Bill smiles at that. "They just better not expect it next year." He puts the plastic shopping bag down, signaling that he's ready to talk. "Not much to tell really. I was out on the Tarmac bringing in a 737. The usual, doing a little dance with my wands, but the pilot isn't paying attention to my instructions. Instead, he's flashing his lights at me. You know, funny stuff goes through your mind, like maybe he's got a hijacker on board or he's having a heart attack. So, finally I look around for the rest of the crew. Instead of guys with ear protectors on the Tarmac with me, I got a Jesus huge polar standing behind me up on his back legs. Swear to god, he's no more than a couple of yards away. So, I make a run for it and duck under the plane I was marshaling. Not like he couldn't follow me, but the pilot revs the engines. Bear decides if this big bird is my momma, he doesn't want anything to do with her."

He reclaims the bag of candy. "Pretty usual stuff up here, you know, with the bears. Us ground crew guys, we all keep a change of underwear in our lockers."

Allsun laughs. "Emergency gear!"

"Yeah, you got it."

"How long did you have to stay under there?" Allsun asks, wondering just how afraid of jet planes a polar bear might be.

"Once those engines were revved up, the bear loped away pretty smart." Bill checks his watch. "Gotta go. Nice meeting you."

"Thanks, Bill. You might want to get security to walk you to your truck with that bag of goodies," Conrad jokes as they make their way down the corridor.

CONRAD'S BRONCO IS a box of dry heat by the time they get inside. Mother Ford makes better than average truck heaters.

Conrad lets Richard out at the Arctic Inn, but not before arrangements are made to meet later at the Legion for a beer. As they watch Rowan disappear into the narrow entryway, where guests have met polar bears on occasion, Conrad offers Allsun a choice of photo ops. "What do you want to see first ... the dump or the jail?"

"You make this sound like an archeological dig in an unfriendly country." Allsun looks out the vehicle window to check the light.

"Just call me Indie." Conrad laughs at himself.

"Let's hit the dump. I assume I'll need a flash for the bear jail." Allsun has got her camera out as they drive a road that must remind Conrad of Saskatchewan: dead flat, open land in all directions. Allsun voices this comparison.

"Yes, there's that," Conrad says. "In some ways this town's not much different from Dinsmore or Strathmore. We Cains always went for 'more.' My old man left the family farm at Strathmore after the war. Bought the place near Dinsmore. There ever since."

"Strathmore, Alberta?"

"Yeah, I don't remember much about it. Did my growing up in Saskatchewan."

"Strathmore. My grandfather ranched there." Allsun gives Conrad a look that says they've just found buried treasure.

"I'll be damned. Small world." Conrad confirms a Canadian truth: big land, not so many people.

"My grandfather died the year I was born. I never saw the place, the homestead. But my dad liked to tell the story of how they dug, by hand, a huge basement, walled it with hand-mixed cement and hand-picked rocks from the pastures, then built the largest house and barn in the district. My grandmother was right in there with her husband and older sons. My grandfather's cattle brand was T9B ... Tom's nine boys ... and four girls. I did the math once: my dad was only three years old when the house was built. He probably remembered next to none of it. I think that's why he liked to tell the story so much. It put him there." Allsun realizes she's doing a lot of the talking. That's what happens when you get going on family. The stories come out. The chain of voices that link you to a larger time.

"We're coming up on the dump," Conrad says.

It's not hard to spot. "A boil on Mother Earth's backside" is what Allsun's grandmother would have called it, speaking of family. There's a mountain of metal, scorched and rusted. In one corner sits a small lake of undulating oil drums. The bears ignore this landscape, intent on digging up household garbage spread about by a bulldozer that has done a poor job of shoveling earth over the mess. Most of the bears have large numbers painted on their sides, which, for some strange reason, makes Allsun think of BINGO. Under the B, 2, "bingo," a bad bear. Watching these magnificent animals foraging in piles of trash shames her.

"This is culture shock," she remarks to Conrad. "From the Cape to this."

"Yeah, culture." His tone is a mix of sarcasm and despair. "Don't get me wrong, I'm proud of Churchill … the way people here try to live with the bears. But this," Conrad waves a hand over the wasteland, "this isn't about Churchill. It's about the world we live in."

"Mankind's clever little hands, making and making …"

"And using." Conrad points to the camera resting in Allsun's lap, then slaps the steering wheel of his Bronco.

"I know, we do our part." The camera remains idle in her lap. Allsun is reluctant to shoot any of this, to fragment and magnify it.

"I don't think the solution is to build landfill sites and incinerators. But what then?" Conrad puts the Bronco in gear as a curious bear approaches them.

"In a way, the Greens are right. We shouldn't be in the North until we know how to live here." Allsun raises the camera to photograph a young bear, standing, its blackened paws resting on the hood of the Ford. "Look at its paws. What's it been into?" she asks Conrad from behind the camera.

"I'll show you." He honks the horn as the bear stretches along the hood trying to get a good look at them through the windshield. This bowlegged bandit doesn't respond. It is intent on them and impervious to everything else. Conrad shifts into reverse and backs away. The bear slides off the vehicle, not without leaving claw marks in Conrad's paint job.

They drive around the piled-up debris to find a fire on the other side. Immediately Allsun starts shooting, holding her breath as she squeezes off shots, a conditioned response from her biathlon days.

It's a scene of black and white and flames. The horizon is a tangle of charred refuse partially covered with snow, a backdrop for six polar bears and a bonfire of modern vanities. The flames are a golden-red curiosity the bears regard as an inconvenience. Fire is not part of their world; they treat it with indifference, singeing their fur as they winkle out bits of food from burning pizza boxes and melting bread bags. The largest bears dominate with open-mouthed growls and swaying heads. It's not a party.

NEITHER IS THE polar bear jail. Right now, it's full of inmates. The Bear Patrol, made up of Natural Resources Officers, the Mounties and volunteer firefighters, have been combing the town and its perimeter. Those bears making it into town are tranquilized and jailed. Those foraging nearby are driven away with flare guns.

"October thirty-first," Conrad says. "All the pagans are rounded up. I'm assuming bears are pagans."

They've entered a cement block building that has

room for twenty-five bears in cells with steel-barred drop gates, portcullis-style. What Allsun notices, even before she focuses on bears chewing the bars on their jail doors, is the drop in temperature and the rise in stench—the rank sweetness of a dog kennel, the miasma of meat-eaters.

She photographs animals that are kind enough to show a lot of teeth. The ones that aren't pacing, that is. The better adjusted, those that have been in awhile, simply sleep.

"It smells like carnivore in here, but there's no whale or seal meat stink." Allsun speaks from behind the camera.

"They don't get food, just water." Conrad sounds morose.

"Convicts in solitary confinement do better than that." She lowers the camera to examine Conrad. This change of mood surprises her.

"No point. You feed them; they come back for more. They're in fasting mode anyway, so it doesn't hurt them to go without food. That's the reasoning." It's obvious Conrad doesn't like being in this building. Is it the caged bears or just the cages?

"Well, what's next?" Allsun opens her jacket and stuffs the camera suspended from her neck inside, away from the cold.

Conrad turns on a dime and makes for the door. "There's lots. What about the Eskimo Museum, the Arctic Trading Company, the Arctic Sewing Centre ... we could go into the workroom where they make parkas, mukluks, moccasins. Or drive out to see Miss Piggy or the Ithaca?"

By now they're at Conrad's Bronco and he hasn't paused but once for breath. Mind, it's wise to keep breathing to a minimum in air rarefied by extreme cold. Allsun waits until they're inside the Ford to ask, "Miss Piggy?"

"A C-46 freight plane that crashed north of the airport a few years ago."

"And?"

"Oh, the Ithaca is another wreck. A beached cargo freighter." Conrad is waiting for a decision before he pulls out and heads down the main street that runs straight through town.

"Churchill sure has its share of disasters." Allsun is buying time as she assesses what might make a story. "Well, a choice of artifacts, huh? What's in the trading post?"

"More art-in-fact," Conrad says this casually as he adjusts the heat to defrost the windows that are collecting their breath.

"Arc-tic-art?" Allsun wastes some more breath. Before Conrad can respond in kind, she tells him, "Enough. Take me to the Post."

"You want to hear something funny?" He reverses out of the parking lot. "Miss Piggy flew for LAMBAIR." Conrad stares at her until she gets it.

Once he sees the light bulb go on above her head, he turns his attention back to the road. Lucky for them it hadn't taken her long to get the joke.

"You should meet Keith Rawlings," he says after they've passed a huge metal sign in Hallowe'en orange declaring POLAR BEAR ALERT STOP DON'T WALK IN THIS AREA. The arresting symbol among the words is a five-toed, five-clawed polar bear paw. Just who is being alerted here: man or beast?

"Now there's a bear lover if there ever was one," Conrad says.

"What?"

"Keith Rawlings . . . he's likely to quote bear poetry at you."

"That might be an improvement on our puns." Allsun is still musing on the orange sign.

She watches the main street go by like the grainy black and white movies that belonged in her grandmother's tin canisters. Buildings are ghosted by spindrift snow, the tops of power lines emerging like rows of dark crosses from the gray-out. The light has become as flat as the landscape.

They pull up to a building floating on waves of wind-driven snow like some sort of ship with its cabin lights on. Above the door is a painted sign—*ARCTIC TRADING COMPANY*—in large, red Tiffany letters arranged below figures that could be from the Cyrillic alphabet.

As if reading Allsun's mind or perhaps the quizzical look on her face, Conrad explains, "It's native. The syllabic system of writing."

"What language?" she asks.

"Well, I guess you'd call it Canadian Eskimo. The Oblate, Arthur Thibert, he calls it that in his dictionary." Conrad scrutinizes the sign for clues to a linguistic history he's not entirely sure of.

"Nice," Allsun says. "And the clipper ship logo . . . two worlds meeting, I guess."

"Wait till you see inside." Conrad throws the door of the Bronco open against the wind.

See! Sight is not the point of reference here, it's smell. And smell it does, of smoke-tanned hides: the sweetness of sugar stored and released in burning logs. Allsun automatically thinks of caramelized brown sugar—hides with the same rich colour and essence. The pot-bellied stove adds its own pungency.

The shelves are lined with fur-trimmed mukluks, beaded moccasins, fur hats, mitts, gauntlets, soapstone sculptures, caribou and moose hair tufting, porcupine quill work, bone carvings. It's an overwhelming display of northern material culture.

Animals reduced to one dimension, skin and fur, appendages splayed out as if caught from behind by a steamroller. Rugs. Animals restored to three-dimensional wall mounts—heads only. Allsun's gaze is captured by the open-mouthed stare of a polar bear rolled inside a glass cabinet, a rug with full head mount. She shifts her focus away from glassy eyes that are nothing like the real thing she has experienced at the Cape. These are no more than fancy buttons on a fur coat.

Next to the polar bear rug is the most exquisitely beautiful piece of clothing she has ever seen. For a better look, Allsun pushes aside an arctic wolf pelt displayed on top of the glass cabinet. The long canid guard hairs under her hand remind her of her dogs, hers and Damon's. The dogs now live on her sister's ranch. She visits Damon. She visits the dogs.

Allsun moves away from the disturbing reassurance of the wolf fur and peers into the cabinet. Laid out on a glass shelf is a magnificent woman's parka, a traditional *amautik*. The body of what is essentially a jacket with a hood has a long curved back panel that would reach to the back of the wearer's knees with a fine fringe tentacling to the calf. The front panel is a similar oblong shape rising to curve at the hip and fall to mid thigh, the fringe extending to the knee. The hood is another ovoid that drapes down the back to below the waist. Decorated with a beaded-fringe border and a panel of fine beadwork expressing an even finer artistic vision, the hood is perhaps the best designed and appointed baby carrier to be found. Hundreds of thousands of glass beads form simple images of complex skill. All this color laid down on a pure white animal hide.

Allsun is squatting, nose against the glass side of the cabinet, and looking up through the glass shelf at the underside of the *amautik*, when she hears a voice behind her.

"Belongs in a museum," the voice tells her.

She stands and turns to face a man with a dark, imposing mustache and laughing eyes. "Is it old?" she asks.

"No, just rare. The beadwork alone took four years. People aren't doing that kind of work much anymore."

"The dark purple glass beads as background for blue, yellow, pink ... I've never seen anything like it. An individual eye for color, I'd say." Allsun stares through the cabinet top at imagined beauty. Then she notices the man's reflection in the glass.

"It took a long time for Elizabeth Nootarauloo to collect the beads," he continues. "Not like the old days, when her husband got paid in beads for the furs he traded to the Hudson's Bay Company."

"What kind of hide has she used?" Allsun looks past the bands of decoration to the *amautik* itself.

"Summer caribou. She tanned and bleached it, cut everything, even the fringe, with an ulu ... you know, the half-moon woman's knife. It's all authentic." The fingers of his right hand stroke the fine fur of the arctic wolf pelt as if it were a dog at his side.

"Yes, I noticed the hair had been left on the hide and turned to the inside of the parka. I don't know, it might take some getting used to, having that hair against your skin."

"At forty below, it might just be a comfort." He nods in agreement with himself.

Conrad has decided to abandon the pot-bellied stove, his features flushed, which only serves to highlight the marks of winter on his face—patches of skin bleached by frostbite and overrun with the spider tracks of broken blood vessels. "Oh, so you two have met?" He rubs his hands together to sustain the warmth he had drawn from the stove.

"No, not really. Just admiring—"

"Well, Allsun Skelly, this is our very own Governor of the Arctic Trading Company, Keith Rawlings." Conrad makes short work of introductions.

Allsun extends her hand. "Should I call you Guv?"

"Accent's still showing, eh? After all these years." Keith has an honest handshake.

"How many years is that?" Allsun asks. There are always stories to be had.

"Came out to Canada in the 'fifties. Cooked for a construction crew in the Northwest Territories," he offers a small piece of the puzzle.

Allsun decides to see what he will do with a less than stock response. "A man after my own heart," she says.

"How's that?" Color creeps up around his ears.

"Cookery, Keith. A guy that can cook gets extra points, especially if he can cook for a crowd." Allsun notices Conrad shift from foot to foot as if relieved to know she's just having a bit of fun.

"In that case," Conrad interjects, "we have to have supper at the Trader's Table. It's Keith and Penny's restaurant."

"Sounds good to me. Conrad and I had a fine lunch of M&M's and Aero bars." She is still watching Conrad, wondering if he really thought she had been coming on to Keith. And if she was, why would it matter to Conrad?

"Got a few things to do before that." Conrad gets them back on track. He leads the way to the door.

While the Arctic Trading Post seems to have raised Conrad's spirits—brought down by the steel bars of the drop gates at the polar bear jail—the inmates of the trading post have left Allsun with a feeling of despair. As much as she loves northern culture, Allsun has never reconciled to the trade in wild animals—dead or alive.

They do a whirlwind tour of the town, slowed only by a rioting wind bent on downing them when they get out of Conrad's vehicle, first at the Arctic Sewing Centre, and then at the Eskimo Museum. Eventually, Conrad stops in front of the Legion Hall. "Take the truck," he says to Allsun. "Go on down to the hospital. I'll bend an elbow with Richard. You can come back and collect us."

ALLSUN'S BOOTS SQUEAL rudely as she makes her way along the highly polished linoleum floor of a hospital corridor. Embarrassed, she passes quiet rooms. At the end of the hall sits an old woman in a white hospital gown and blue cotton robe. A long black tail of hair hangs limply over one shoulder of the robe with its cross-hatched pattern and navy blue trim. As Allsun reaches the end of the corridor, she notices the tattoos on the face, arms and hands of the old Inuit woman. The blue lines on her face are crosshatched by profound wrinkles. Columns of indigo blue lines, as straight as text, march stanza-like down each arm to the first knuckles of strong hands slightly distorted by arthritis. The nail of her right index finger is the caramel color of the nicotine she's being denied in this place. The woman smiles and nods.

Allsun rounds a corner, the woman is lost, and Neal is found. "I hear you're making trouble," she greets him.

His eyes fly open. "If it isn't Florence Nightingale in SnowPaks. Guy send you to talk some sense into me?"

"How did you guess?" Allsun sits in the chair beside Neal's bed, lifts one foot then the other out of the heavy, felt-lined boots. Thrusting out her long legs, she wiggles her toes in a show of sublime freedom.

"He's a born worrier."

"Papa Bear." Allsun grins.

"I got work to do." Neal is not about to go down memory lane with Allsun. "The bear spray could be an important breakthrough. Something everyone could use. It might even replace guns in the camps. I need to get these tests done."

"Okay, okay, fine by me. But you know I've got orders to talk to the doc."

"Talk to anyone you want. I'm outta here tomorrow." He crosses his arms over his chest.

"How come you're such a hardass? I've come all the way to Churchill to see you and all I get is grief." Allsun stares down the crossed arms.

The word *grief* stings Neal. An image of Allsun in Damon's hospital room shames him. "Sorry, Al. This can't be easy for you."

"This," she underscores the word, "isn't easy for any of us. What did you think would happen when the three of us got back together?"

Neal is not prepared for her question. "I don't know. I wasn't thinking of it that way. I'm working with Guy now on the Bear Safety Program and I thought . . . you needed a break."

"But it's the Cape, Neal." Allsun is not convinced that this is all there is to her presence at the camp. "What about Jane? Is she still here?"

"No. Ancient history." He knows better than to take his eyes off her face.

She is not fooled. "You called me Jane."

"What? I wouldn't—"

"When I pulled you out of the Tundra Buggy."

"Yeah, well I was gassed, out of my mind. Believe me, I know . . ." Neal studies a face he has come to see in his dreams more often than Jane's face. And he's not entirely sure why. "I . . . Jane isn't real to me anymore. Not even at the Cape."

Allsun senses there is more to his claim, but for some reason she is afraid to pursue it. Instead, she makes reassuring noises and feels like a phony. She can't help but notice how good she's become at plying platitudes that sound sincere, are sincere on one level, the least satisfying level, band-aids on gaping wounds.

Dr. Thomas finds his way into Neal's room, scattering her thoughts with an opening volley, "So how are my reluctant patients? Time to talk turkey."

Neal and Allsun exchange looks.

"Propane: C_3H_8, boiling point –42°C. The third in the alkane series of hydrocarbons, a gas obtained from petroleum and natural gas, used as a fuel and a refrigerant. That's what we know. In humans, inhalation causes central nervous system disorder and/or damage, irritation, cardiac arrhythmias, breathing failure, coma and death. This we also know. What we don't know is the long-term consequences of getting a lungful of propane. Both of you should have more tests done. When you were admitted yesterday, we did blood chemistry, white cell count, that kind of thing. Besides administering oxygen and an intravenous infusion of 5 percent dextrose in saline, you haven't given us much of a chance to deal with your condition."

"My nose burns and my throat is really sore, but otherwise I don't feel too bad." Neal looks to Allsun. "I can't speak for both of us, but I need to get back to work. Can the tests wait?"

Dr. Thomas contemplates them in silence. He stands and turns toward the door.

Neal and Allsun glance at each other.

The doctor looks back at them. "Lend me your bodies for the rest of the afternoon and then we'll see. Deal?"

THE RED SUN has flatlined on the horizon. Allsun walks out of a breathtaking cold dusk into choking cigarette smoke. The Legion beer hall is another world. She locates Conrad and Richard at one of many hubcap-size tables. The orange terry cloth-covered top supports several rounds of empty beer glasses.

Conrad offers her his chair. As she slides it toward Richard Rowan, Conrad snags another from a nearby table, completing the circle. "How's Neal?" he asks.

"Seems okay." Allsun catches the waitress's eye. "Another round and black coffee with a shot of Southern Comfort for me." To the men she says, "I'm sick to death of tea."

Richard nods, either in agreement with Allsun or at the waitress. He turns to Allsun. "Conrad told me what happened. You're pretty lucky."

"Good thing I'm a light sleeper ... years of practice." Allsun pulls off her toque, causing static electricity to swirl loosened hairs in the air around her head like magnetized filaments.

Conrad is captivated by this coppery light show.

Richard steeples the fingers of both hands. "Seems to me there's been a lot of accidents at the Cape in the last few days."

"I meant to ask you, Richard," Conrad resists the desire to place his hands in the chaos around Allsun's head, "how the latch looked when you entered the observation cage?"

"Fine, I guess." He contemplates his fingers. "Just shot it closed, didn't look real close. Had some ice on it."

"Ice?" Conrad repeats. He studies the last inch of shandy in his glass. "Now why would that be?"

The waitress arrives. Allsun hands up empty glasses to clear a spot for her coffee and the new round. "Remember, the cage was moved. Jud used water to freeze the bottom to the ground. Keep it in place." Allsun glances at Richard. "Not that it stayed put once Richard's bear got playful."

"Not much did," Richard doesn't look up, "including my innards . . . flopping around in my throat trying to escape." He raises his head and smiles shyly, as if he's just left the confessional.

"For Guy's sake, I hope things go smoothly from here on in. It's been a tough fall." Conrad tracks the bubbles to the surface of the pale liquid in his glass.

"How's that?" Richard is careful not to sound too interested. Despite the glasses he has emptied, he's still a journalist asking questions, and an American journalist to boot.

Like a true Canadian, Conrad cites the weather. "Freeze-up's early this year. Good for the bears, bad for bear research."

Richard tries a different line of inquiry. "I read in one of your newspapers that the federal government's environment department is under review. How does that play out here?"

Conrad lifts his glass. "Don't know. You'd have to ask Guy."

"I understand Neal's from the private sector?" Richard directs this question to Allsun.

"Oil and gas," Allsun replies, interested to see how another journalist works up material.

"And the three of you are friends?" Richard points at his empty glass as the waitress swings by.

"University." Allsun remains elusive, letting him angle.

"You did biology?" Richard appears confused.

"No, my husband. The three of them were graduate students." Allsun follows the retreating back of the waitress with her eyes, hoping she will remember to bring the coffee pot when she returns, then brings her eyes to the table in time to catch Conrad's full gaze on her face.

"Your husband's not part of this research?" Richard is watching Conrad.

"He's not part of this world."

"Sorry?" Richard looks from Conrad to Allsun.

"My husband's in a coma. Attacked . . . by a group called LIB." Allsun decides she wants more than coffee.

"LIB." Startled, Richard tries to compose his face. "I didn't . . . I'm sorry."

Conrad detects the note of recognition in Richard's voice.

The waitress returns with another beer for Richard, who seems relieved. Allsun orders a double screwdriver. It's on the waitress's tray when she makes her next sweep by minutes later.

They sit in silence. Richard studies his beer; Conrad studies Richard.

Slightly addled—by alcohol or adrenaline, he's not sure which—Richard reassesses what he knows of Jud Ash and LIB. The latest piece of the puzzle was delivered in a phone conversation he had just hours ago: he was told Jud Ash struck a man with a tire iron during a raid on the vivarium at the University of Calgary.

Richard is the first to speak. "Did they catch the guy?" he asks Allsun.

"What?" Allsun is caught in her own thoughts. With the help of the screwdriver, she has pried up a corner of the lid she had slammed down on her future. Before she can look in, she's overcome by a powerful wave of sexual excitement. She's so stunned, she goes blank.

"Your husband's attacker? Was he prosecuted?"

Allsun is flung back into the smoky room by the sound of Richard's voice. "No . . . don't know who did it."

Conrad spots Allsun's disorientation. "Let's get some supper," he says to the others.

Richard waves a hand at the waitress and imitates signing a bill. "Gotta go back to the hotel. Wait for a call."

DINNER AT THE Trader's Table is enough comfort to make a person forget the world of snow and sub-zero temperatures outside. Wine and a good meal have Allsun and Conrad trading adventure stories—cross-country ski trips, cross-country dog sled trips, overnighting in snow caves, in igloos—and so it goes.

Conrad decides to move the conversation to common ground. "So you grew up on a ranch?"

"No." Allsun is confused by his question. "I was raised in Calgary, but my dad made sure us kids learned to ride. What made you think—"

"Strathmore—"

"Oh, no, my grandparents lost the homestead during the Great Depression. Tom's nine boys got work where they could. A few of my uncles rode the rails. One made the On to Ottawa Trek." Allsun pauses to remember. "Maggie and her four girls took in washing and did hair-dressing, I think. My grandfather never went back to the land."

Conrad spreads his paper napkin on the table and takes out a pen. He draws two overlapping squares, two interlocking circles, a grid, and a figure eight cat with a smile. Pushing the paper toward her, he asks, "Recognize this?"

"Your first geometry lesson?"

"Yeah, a kind of geometry. One of my uncles taught me the language used during the Depression by the unemployed men who went from town to town looking for work. They carried a piece of chalk and left messages for those coming behind, usually warnings about hostile residents, guard dogs, police." Conrad considers what he has written.

Allsun nods at the white napkin stained red by the light from a candle contained in a ruby glass jar. "What does it say?"

Conrad points to each symbol. "Afraid, Don't give up, Jail, Good Woman."

Allsun tries to connect the symbols with the words. The only one that makes sense to her is the grid representing jail. Suddenly she realizes she's staring at a sentence, a message. She raises her head to look at Conrad. The expression on his face is one she hasn't seen for a long time.

He reaches for her hand and accidentally knocks over her coffee cup. A brown stain spreads, creating an island on the white linen ocean between them.

Allsun stares at the overturned cup. Damon had knocked over her coffee that first meeting in the Jungle and covered his embarrassment by launching into a witty send-up of the half full/half empty theory of life. At the end of his lampoon, they had talked seriously about life.

Conrad blots the stain with his paper napkin, the napkin he had drawn on just minutes ago. The signs of desperate men bleed away.

Allsun's message has been erased, but not before she has read into it, support for her decision. She'll go home to Damon and ensure his future.

The waiter has come by with a new napkin and the coffee pot. Conrad rights Allsun's cup. The waiter pours. Conrad realizes that Allsun has retreated. "Sorry for the mess," he says to her.

"Sorry?"

"I ruined—"

"Don't worry. It'll be alright."

THE SHOCK OF being out on the street reverberates through Allsun and Conrad in shivers that would register on the Richter scale. Allsun is beginning to regret her suggestion of walking to the Town Complex's community center. Nevertheless, on the way, she hopes to photograph the trick and treaters with their armed guards.

Under the sickly orange-yellow of streetlights are gangs with face masks and shopping bags. Trussed up in snowsuits against the cold, they all look like overfed goblins, ghosts and witches. Those who are aware of the padded, rounding-out effect of their attire have chosen bear masks. More than half of the kids Allsun photographs are disguised as polar bears—part of the psyche of this town. It's not the dead they fear. In the background of most of her shots are parents in cars and trucks.

The community hall in the Town Complex is full of high-ceiling noise all centered on a gigantic wooden polar bear that would put the Trojan Horse to shame.

Not unlike the ancient Greeks, and in an unnatural reversal of peristalsis, children climb into the arse end of the bear and spew themselves out of its mouth by way of a red tonguish slide. Costumes are strewn on benches and chairs like so many casualties, while parents sit nearby guarding the bags of loot.

Conrad introduces Allsun around and she asks permission to take photographs.

Later, retreating from the chaos, she buys a cup of coffee at the concession and joins Conrad, who is holding an animated conversation with Bishop Robidoux.

"Allsun, I tell you, this man has lived all these years in the wilderness and I still can't get him to agree with Matthew Fox." Conrad pulls her into their debate without missing a beat.

"Who?" is as much of a response as she can muster.

"You must have heard about him in the news?" Conrad succeeds in adding to her puzzlement.

Bishop Robidoux sees Allsun's confusion as an opportunity. "That Dominican out of California who gets himself in trouble on a regular basis."

"What good's a theologian who doesn't question," Conrad opens his hands palms up, "especially the status quo?"

Bishop Robidoux smiles knowingly at Conrad's opening of arms and showing of palms. "To suggest that we must reinvent Christianity is more than questioning . . ." Conrad makes to interject but the Bishop holds up a hand, "and then to suggest the blueprint for this renovating of the rock, well, that's the man speaking, not the priest."

" 'Mother earth is dying' . . . and that's as good a point

of departure as any for a new look at how we live. Religion is part of living . . . can't be left out of the equation." Conrad crosses his arms over his chest. "That's basically what Fox is saying."

The Bishop counters, "I think you're oversimplifying the issue." Then he turns to Allsun. "This is not a new discussion for us, it can wait for another day." He very neatly pulls the plug on Conrad.

The rest of the conversation becomes something of an interview as Allsun fleshes out another kind of northerner. Bishop Robidoux' diocese covers 3.8 million square kilometers involving him with a great many Inuit. What's on his mind as they speak is the anti-fur lobby. He has cast his lot with the northern fur traders, many of whom are his friends. Allsun plays devil's advocate, when, in fact, she's a fence-sitter on this issue. There is no simple solution here. She was reminded of that earlier today when she visited the Arctic Trading Company.

BACK IN CONRAD'S truck, Allsun expects to be dropped off at the Arctic Inn. As Conrad pulls out onto Kelsey Boulevard, his face turned to nonexistent traffic on a street as straight as a trapline leading out onto the tundra, he offers her his spare room. "It's not much, but you're welcome to it," he says.

"That's really nice of you," Allsun stalls. There it is again, the same thrill that went through her body in the Legion Hall. "Yeah, okay . . . thanks." She's smiling when he looks at her.

They are on their way out of town and headed for Conrad's home. The last sign Allsun is able to read in the blowing snow stands in front of the Holy Canadian Martyrs Church: the notice board announces GUILT SHOW, OCT 31–NOV 10. "Did you see that?" she asks Conrad.

"What?"

"The sign in front of the Catholic Church."

"No. Why?"

"You should see this."

Conrad hits the brakes and spins a one-eighty on the icy street. He drives right up to the sign, fixing it in his headlights. He laughs. "Oh that's rich. The pagans are out tonight. The Bishop will get a charge out of this, if the quilters don't get to it before he sees it."

As they drive to his home, Conrad recounts the days of Fort Churchill, the joint Canada and U.S. military installation dating back to 1942 and predicated on claims of German submarines sighted in the Hudson Strait. When the military arrived, Churchill had a population of 150 people. There were more bears than townsfolk. Churchill was an outpost with no utilities: no running water, sewers, streetlights. Then, thousands of servicemen and hundreds of civilian personnel descended like squadrons of mosquitoes and deer flies—the northern plague. In this case, instead of sucking the lifeblood of the town, the influx provided a transfusion: new money, new resources, government attention.

"Base shut down in the 'sixties. No more Siberia, American-style. The troops left, I think, with few regrets. More regrets for the town, obviously." Conrad pays little attention to a road he has driven countless times, other than to remark that it wouldn't be here if it weren't for the rocket range.

Allsun is still interested in the base. "How many able-bodies are we talking about?"

"I've been told somewhere around 4,500 servicemen and support staff."

"Up here? Why? I mean, other than the Second World War scare, why would you put those kinds of resources into here for twenty-two years?" The journalist in Allsun is pondering a military installation the size of Fort Churchill in the middle of nowhere—what kind of research could have been done out there, far from prying eyes?

"Substitute Russian subs for German subs and all the Commy stuff in the States. I think the Red Scare kept the Fort in place." Conrad doesn't seem to be on the same train of thought as Allsun. Her train has more of the Orient Express about it, careening from Istanbul to Paris, the seats full of spies.

She doesn't give voice to her private speculations. Instead, she says, "Think of all the government money put into that place before and after the war."

"Ain't that the truth. But Public Works did use the base until it was bulldozed in 1981. Left us the airstrip and hangars so the town would have an airport." Conrad adjusts his steering by degrees—a tiller in the stiff northern wind—to keep them on the perfectly straight road.

"What did Public Works do with a base that size?" Allsun is barely aware of the landscape changing beyond the frosted windows, her mind engaged in working out how to research Fort Churchill.

"Scientific studies," Conrad says casually.

"Oh, like what?" She hasn't failed to notice that Conrad got on her Orient Express at the last stop in the conversation.

"Don't know. Kept that stuff to themselves. Came and went without setting foot in town." Now on board, Conrad is playing at inscrutability.

"That's interesting. Might be worth looking into, maybe a story there." Instinctively Allsun downplays this statement, a journalist's habit long ingrained.

"It's probably classified." Conrad's tone says he's not buying her disinterest.

"There are ways." Now she's donning the trench coat and slouch hat of spy vs. spy. Next, her nose will grow cartoonishly long and pointy like the noses of the spies of *MAD Magazine*.

"I don't know." Conrad has a look in his eyes that should gives rise to a balloon caption above his head with the word *devilish* in it. "Might've been connected to Defense, since they also held maneuvers here and did survival training."

"Survival training? Winter or summer?" Allsun shoots back.

"Mostly winter, I think. Why?" Conrad responds with surprise.

"I wonder . . ." She's trying to focus, to put together scraps of memory as if taping together a torn page. "Damon worked with one of the professors at the University of Calgary's medical school on hypothermia, particularly cold-water immersion. Damon was mostly a human guinea pig . . . submerged in ice water. He was just beginning to develop a serious interest in wilderness survival and he wanted to know everything he could about winter survival, everything, especially how much cold he could take."

"But what's that got—"

"I'm not sure. This was a while ago, when he was an undergraduate student. But there was something to do with research done by the Nazis in the concentration camps during the war. Data was recovered that showed German scientists were studying cold-water hypothermia. I guess their methods were pretty grim. They put men and women in ice-water vats and recorded every stage of hypothermia until they died. The researchers documented everything meticulously, starting with complete preliminary physicals, registering height, weight, age, physical condition and race." Recalling this, Allsun is no longer inclined to think of government-employed agents as characters in thrillers or comic books.

Conrad is listening carefully, interested in what she has to say, but even more interested to hear her speak of her husband. "Christ, I've been in the water out there." He nods toward the Bay. "What a horrible way to die."

"Makes you wonder, doesn't it? Just what kind of animal we are?" An involuntary shiver seizes her by the neck. "I remember that one of the categories was called 'physical activity' and it had to do with how completely a 'subject' was restrained in the water ... how much they were allowed to move to keep themselves warm."

"But I still don't get your drift about—"

"That data ... the results from the concentration camp experiments ... not long after it was discovered, it went missing and didn't turn up again until some time in the 'seventies. Where was it all those years? Was some government analyzing it?"

"To what end?" This is less a question from Conrad than an exclamation.

"I don't know. It's about as obvious as why the Canadian and American military spent twenty-two years here, in northern Canada. Maybe the Cold War was ice cold. Maybe they thought the earth's skullcap—"

"The what?"

"The north pole . . . was going to be the next battleground. Russian invasion across the top of the world."

"Geez, you've got some kind of mind, putting that together. Do you believe it?"

"What's to believe?" Allsun is reminded that Conrad is not in her kind of business. "Just educated speculation." Looking out the window, she notices among the pothole lakes a strange configuration of even stranger buildings.

Conrad glances at her. "More mysterious installations," he says in a conspiratorial whisper.

"Silos, by the looks of them, and not for storing grain," she remarks, trying to decide if Conrad is mocking her.

But what gives the scene an alien quality is the miles of above-ground metal tunnels connecting the buildings with geometric precision. Gray tunnels form a triangle. There's a gray tunnel star with a silo at each of its points.

"Rockets, U.S. Air Force, NASA, NRC . . . What do you think?" Conrad is acting like the spy who came in from the cold.

"Weather." Allsun almost adds *nothing more arcane.* "Weather research."

"Yeah, over 3,400 rocket launches. I was there for the final one on May 8th," Conrad says with unexpected emotion. "Sure hated to see those people leave. Got to know a few of them pretty well."

Allsun can see how. They are barely past the outskirts

of the silent rocket range when they turn down a road cut through some black spruce. Conrad shifts into four-wheel drive to plow through snowdrifts contained and protected by the trees. They emerge from the scrubby windbreak at an A-frame house set into a small hill above a frozen lake.

Conrad's home is not exactly small, but it seems self-contained in the manner of an aircraft. What strikes Allsun as she studies the timber and tin roof house are the large windows, none of which have curtains. Mind you, hidden out here, there's no need to keep the world out.

Since he's a guy living alone, she expects to see all the latest toys, assuming he has a decent power supply. As they walk into his living room, Allsun is not disappointed. It's full of gadgets, most of which are pointing out two huge windows. Telescopes. Serious telescopes. Serious windows for a cold clime.

"You sure those sky scientists went home? Looks like they're living with you." Allsun acknowledges what most probably brings Conrad home at night.

"Only in spirit. Well, and a few odds and ends of equipment." Conrad tries not to look too pleased with his little observatory.

"What have you got here?" Allsun is sincerely interested. She too has a soft spot for tubes fitted out with lenses. Instruments of sight and insight.

"This big baby is my pride and joy." Conrad doesn't touch the telescope, but if he could hug it without disturbing it, he would. "A Schmidt-Cassegrain. It's a compound telescope, portable but with great light-gathering ability. It also takes photographs."

"Looks like you've got it set up with a timer." She was hooked before he mentioned photography.

"Yeah, she's been working while I was away," Conrad says with affection.

Allsun watches Conrad check the Schmidt-Cassegrain. There's nothing like a machine, she thinks, that works on our behalf when we're not present, to elicit our devotion. Is it akin to the invisible hand of a god or the unconditional caring of a mother?

She moves toward what can only be described as a contraption. "What's this monster?"

"That's a hand-built Newtonian telescope. First one I made. It's got a fifteen-centimeter mirror that I had to shape." Of course there is some pride here, but it's guileless. It seems as if Conrad considers these icons, not machines.

"Why the small scope perched on top?" Allsun asks.

"It's a finder telescope. It's got a wider viewing field than the Newt does. Standard stuff. The Schmidt-Cassegrain has one too." He points it out.

In all, Conrad has five telescopes and several tape recorders, for spoken records. These and a workbench sit before the windows. The sloping walls of the A-frame form a cosmic wedge: every square inch right to the pyramid peak is covered with charts, maps, photographs, posters.

Allsun reads captions revealing Jupiter's Great Red Spot, a radar map of Venus, a globular cluster in the constellation Pegasus, the Orion Nebula, the Horsehead Nebula. Such words! What she's attracted to are the reproductions of old atlases. Pegasus from the atlas of Hevelius published in 1690 is precisely rendered from nose to forelegs where the wings attach. This flying horse, fully sketched and shaded, is surrounded by the ephemeral figures of a man constellation—Aquarius; a woman constellation—Andromeda (a long chain tipped like an arrow attached to her wrist); a fish—Piscis Austrinus; and several phantom horses. Behind the recognizable images are stars.

"You really are a sky-person, Conrad," Allsun murmurs, not taking her eyes off the heavens.

"'Sky-person' sounds like something Human Resources at an airline would come up with."

This remark is definitely not in the spirit of things.

"Okay, how about heavenly body?" Allsun counters.

"Now you're trying to make me blush." He laughs. "My friends over the way at NRC really got me started. Before that I was just dilly-dallying around."

When Allsun turns to him, she finds that in fact there is a rosy flush creeping up his neck toward his ears.

"You're sure in the right place—long nights and no city lights." She laughs at her silly rhyme.

"That could be my motto."

"You're welcome to it, copyright granted."

"I've got a few things to check on here." Conrad points to his observatory. "Would you like coffee?"

"Sure, I'll make it." Allsun retraces their steps to the walled-off portion of the main floor. In this part of the house there are two rooms: the kitchen, through which they had entered from outside, and a smaller room to the right of the door, which she discovers is a bathroom, complete with shower.

Conrad gives directions from the living room. "Coffee's in the fridge. Filters in the top right-hand drawer."

Allsun starts the coffee maker and returns to the living

room, where Conrad is perched like a parent crane over one of his sky-watchers.

"Do you mind if I take a shower?" she asks.

"No, by all means. It will be our little secret," he says, without disengaging himself from the telescope.

"Pardon me?"

"At the Cape."

"Yes?"

"Don't want to make them jealous when you get back to camp, do you?" He raises his head and winks.

Allsun laughs. "I won't smell like the rest of the pack! I'll be an outcast!"

"Yeah, but it's your choice."

"I'll take my chances."

YOU HAVE TO want a shower pretty badly to take your clothes off in a house that for days has seen only enough heat to keep the water pipes from freezing. The linoleum on the bathroom floor has worn from white to beige in the center, making it seem as if there is frost on the floor along the walls. She runs the water to get it hot while she undresses—exposing herself on the outside of the shower curtain for seconds only. She's under the running facet for a green-approved five minutes.

Turning the water off, steam rising, she thinks of the Polar Bear Clubs: those people who swim, bath, frolic, call it what you will; those insane people who venture into bodies of water in the northern hemisphere, in the winter; those people who have to hack holes in the ice to frolic in some lake; those people who swim among floating bits of berg in the ocean.

As Allsun gropes for the towel, she wonders why they don't all die of heart attacks. The closest she has come to that kind of extreme-induced fibrillation is diving naked into a mountain lake after leaving the sanctuary of a *wickiup*: a native sauna made from woven willow wands, whatever covering is to hand (hides, blankets, sheet plastic) and hot rocks from the campfire. The thought of the scorching steam off those rocks in the sauna pit sustains her long enough to towel off and get her gooseflesh into her not so clean clothing.

Allsun leaves the rapidly cooling bathroom as Conrad shoves a log into the Elmira Stove Works airtight that dominates the corner between the kitchen and the living room. Elmira's gaping mouth of flame beckons her into the room, where she kneels on the hearth rug, bows and shakes her wet hair into the radiant heat.

Conrad closes the glass doors against sparks. "Coffee's ready. How do you take it?" he asks.

"Black," Allsun says, holding her supplicant posture before the great black box of fire.

She rises, hair damp, face suffused, to find Conrad cutting thick slices of sausage and cheese.

"Try this." He offers meat and cheese on a cracker.

Allsun slides into one of two black leather chairs pulled up within sparking distance of Elmira. "Good stuff." Her praise is heralded by a shower of cracker crumbs.

"Elk." Conrad already has a spray of crumbs down the front of his plaid shirt.

Allsun takes note: he has changed into a clean shirt while she was in the shower. "Never had it done with spices like salami. It's great." She reaches for her coffee off the tray. "You got a recipe? For my sister. She and her husband raise elk on their ranch."

"No fooling? An elk ranch?" Conrad brushes off his shirt front.

"Yup. The demand's been increasing steadily. Especially restaurants." Allsun stretches her feet in their rough woolen socks out to Big Black E.

"They have cattle too?"

"Yeah."

"Keep 'em separate?"

"Oh, yeah. Different diseases. It's becoming a concern." Allsun realizes with a shock that this is the most relaxed she's felt in months, no years.

"That's it." Conrad sounds an authority. "That was the big worry back home when one of the neighbors decided to bring in some buffalo. Raised 'em, crossbred 'em."

"Beefalo, something like that?"

"Yeah, beefalo. Ever tried to round them up?" Conrad asks.

"No, I don't do much riding any more." Allsun is only half listening, while she charts unfamiliar territory. She can't remember the last time she felt like an individual, a person unto herself. It feels good, good and guilty.

"Yeah, the things people get up to." Conrad lets the conversation slip away.

They sit, content to watch the fire. The magician in Elmira sends light and shadows up the pyramid walls where meteors reign and constellations ghost. Allsun lies back in the chair, one of those curved Swedish models that accommodates her motion, to survey Conrad's heaven.

"You could get lost up there," she says, tilted back like an astronaut.

"That's the idea." His voice comes to her through currents of warm air, tinged with fire, red like a storm on Mars.

"You don't strike me as a lost soul." Allsun observes the face of Orion the Hunter instead of Conrad's.

"Lost and found." Conrad and Orion are both nebulous.

"How so?"

"When I built the Newt I thought I wanted to look at the stars. Finally the day came—well, the night—I looked through the eyepiece and looked and looked and it didn't mean a thing. The sky came into focus but heaven didn't."

"What were you looking for?"

"Focus."

"But . . ."

"Not the kind you get from adjusting the scope."

There is a long companionable silence, fire as always a medium. Drawn in, Allsun takes up Conrad's word, *focus*, a word she knows all too well, right down to its Latin root, *hearth*. She smiles at Elmira, imagines her flanked by Lares and Penates—the household gods of the Romans. So, Conrad was looking for a place to dwell, and he looked to the heavens. Nothing too mysterious about that.

"We're all junkies," he says. "To be human is to be a junkie."

This brings her down to earth and back to hearth. "Say again?"

"We grab onto things, like we're drowning. All this debris floating around us . . . big and small. We climb onto the big pieces to stay afloat, take the little pieces with us to occupy our minds ... dull the fear." There is no particular urgency in Conrad's voice.

She tries to reconcile his analogy to this room, this moment. "We're talking about life, right?"

"You've climbed onto photography," he responds, "cling to your cameras, take the edge off your fear with candy."

"So, I'm a what? A gadget freak, image junkie, chocoholic? Well, when you look at it that way . . ."

But Conrad is not. "All the debris floating around us, a lot of it's crap. That's the difference. The sky has always been my passion, so I climbed into the cockpit of airplanes. One of the good pieces floating out there. I made my piece of debris an island and took the bottle with me for company. Not so good."

"And the stars?" she asks, aware that Conrad has invited her onto his island.

"Ah, the stars. I built the Newt instead of going on a binge. You can't be a pilot and a steady drinker. So I binge drank. It's no wonder I didn't see anything when I finally put the scope up to my eye. I'd been looking for something else."

Allsun is almost afraid to ask, but ask she does—she's addicted to knowing. "Which was?"

"Wonder," he says without hesitation. "Over the years, I'd lost the amazement I felt at the sky. I'd put too much into it. Made it my home, my business, and I lost the awe I'd felt." Conrad looks around the room, then up to the ceiling.

"So, you got bigger telescopes?"

"Nope, I bought books. Anything with a reference to sky in the title, including *The Coming of the Cosmic Christ.*"

"Oh, I see." Allsun is on alert. In the last few years Damon's family has tried to make religion as important to her as it is to them.

"There's a lot of debris in books, you know. Some good, some bad. What I finally hauled on board was this, 'A Kioto painter burnt a hole in his roof to admire a moonlight effect, and in his rapt admiration omitted to notice that he had set a whole quarter of the city on fire.'"

She follows Conrad's gaze to *his* ceiling, searching for scorch marks. If there is a hole, it has been patched and hidden under posters of celestial bodies.

"Geez, Conrad, how did you get from astronomy to a Japanese painter? Boggles the mind."

"Through Guy," is his answer.

"Our Guy?"

"The very same. There's more there than meets the eye."

Allsun laughs. "So, what's not apparent about our resident bear biologist?"

"He's a poetry junkie," Conrad says, as if every scientist naturally has a love of poetics.

"Hmm, must be those long winter nights in Inuvik. I don't ever remember Guy reading poetry. So, you got your flotsam and jetsam theory of life from a book of poetry?" Her sense of relief that they are talking about verse, not scripture, makes her statement sound more like banter than she intends.

Conrad looks at Allsun and begins to laugh.

Allsun offers up a tentative chuckle, wondering if she has embarrassed herself. "What kind of poetry?"

"What? Oh, all kinds ...you name it. But it was a book

by Robert Bly—*Leaping Poetry*—that got me thinking. When I was young I leapt into the sky. I lost that ...loss has a funny way of creeping up on you like fog. I didn't know what I was missing, I just felt like an amputee with a phantom limb. There's lots of pain in a phantom limb, you know. Anyway, Bly talks about ... a lot of stuff, really, you almost need to read him to understand. What twigged for me was that he put imagination ahead of reason. I'd been living a rational life like we're taught to do. But a strict diet of reason is no good for you. When you look into the night sky, when you look at the stars, you have to use your imagination. Astronomy is speculation, is association. Bly writes about psychic association, leaping from the conscious to the unconscious and back again. He calls it 'riding the dragon.' That's what I do ... I ride the dragon into the sky."

"Holy smoke, Conrad!"

He laughs, "No . . . dragon smoke . . . 'long tails of dragon smoke.'"

"I don't know what to say. You and Guy must have some incredible discussions out there on the tundra."

"Guy took to *Leaping Poetry* because Bly associates the unconscious with our animal instincts. Guy's interested in the animal in us. Sees poets, some poets, as digging into that part of ourselves we've buried."

Conrad stokes Elmira against the night and offers Allsun a drink against the day. She is aware of the day hunched at the base of her neck between her shoulder blades—an homunculus with burning feet dancing on trigger-point nerves. It's the price she pays for years of hanging pounds of metal around her neck.

Conrad has a selection of fine Scotches, the kind that

are not consumed casually. They sit in companion chairs, tasting fire and watching the flames.

Allsun breaks the comfortable silence. "Given what you and Guy are into, talking to Chuck Ford for two days must have been less than stimulating."

"You might think so, but it had its moments. When he wasn't asking me questions about the rocket range and military activity up here, we argued about religion." Conrad discovers a trail of crumbs leading down to his shirt pocket. Rather than brush them away, he smiles benignly at them. "Ford's born again. He's one of those Billy Graham, evangelist types. He gave me a chance to exercise my ongoing argument with the Bishop."

"No, really?" Allsun swirls the Cragganmore in her glass and inhales the smoky fumes. "How'd you get onto that topic?"

"Permafrost."

"Pardon?"

"I was telling him about tundra tires on fixed wing aircraft ... permafrost makes the tundra pretty rough terrain for landing or taking off, not to mention the pingos. Those mounds of dirt with their cores of ice are like a boulder field."

"Pingos." Allsun repeats the word just for the sound of it on her tongue with the single malt.

"Yeah. Chuck ruminates for awhile and when I think he's getting ready to ask me what a pingo is, he says, 'How do you dig a grave in that shit?'"

"What?"

"What, is right. So, I tell him that it wasn't common practice among the Inuit to bury their dead. They put them out on the land for the animals to take care of. He considers this barbaric. Says even in New Orleans where you can't dig a hole without it filling with ground water, they have the decency to cover their dead, shelter them in tombs away from the likes of animals, wild or not. Like he knows best. That attitude gets up my nose." Conrad reviews all this in the bottom of his glass. "Then I tell him that Christian burial isn't the only way. In fact, I see it as wasteful and devious."

"Whoa! Doing a little baiting?" Allsun speculates as to what makes Conrad so complex. Is it the winters here along the fifty-eighth parallel? Long dark time to foment discontent?

"No, I meant it. To leave your dead for the animals to scavenge is to give back to the creatures that you depend upon for food. To leave your dead above ground is to acknowledge rather than hide them. We need to see the change that death brings, otherwise we become obsessed with what we can't see, with what's happening underground, out of sight. It's a horrible, ambivalent state."

Allsun goes quiet. The Highland smoke she has drunk separates Conrad's words: *underground*, *horrible*, *ambivalent* float before her eyes.

"You want to talk about it?" Conrad asks.

"No, that's the problem; there has been too much talk and not enough action." She doesn't look up from her glass. "Thanks, though."

"I better give our fearless leader at the Cape a call." Conrad rises. "You want another wee dram?" He passes her the bottle on his way to the loft.

As she listens to his radiospeak, she casts around the room looking for something outside herself to settle her mind on. Allsun is drawn to the telescopes. At the window she looks up to the night sky. A charge runs through her like a current burning her to the boards beneath her feet. Northern lights! The spirits of the land leaping into the sky. She grabs her parka, pulls it on and opens the door to the wooden deck beyond the windows.

Conrad finds her bathed in the neon green of an aurora borealis sky. For a moment he stands watching her through the glass door. He knows she could live here. There would be enough wonder for her. Conrad steps out behind her, not bothering with a coat.

"They're not this bright at home," she says to him.

"No." He could explain, but he doesn't.

The cold fills his lungs with a quickening burn. Alive . . . vividly, vitally alive. A powerful entity—the magnetic lights, him, both charged particles. Singular. He's elated and sad.

Conrad looks from the burst of cold flame in the sky to Allsun's face and sees the white blooms. "We should go in," he says, "you've got some frostbite."

Inside, he cups his hands over a spot of paper-white skin on her cheek and blows down the fleshy cone. His breath is warm, tinged with peat smoke. He does the same to a spot on the other cheek, then draws his fingers across her forehead, tracing circles at her temples. His fingers lightly dance across her lids. Her eyes remain closed as his touch finds her lips and trails down the lines at each corner to her chin.

Allsun leans into his chest and cries against his shoulder.

IN THE LOFT the aurora borealis surges around them. The skylight in Conrad's roof is as full of flame as the Kioto painter's. Streamers of green-gold pulse over their skin, wrapping them together in light. The heat is their own.

AT THE CAPE, the northern lights had been the after dinner entertainment. Guy had done the cooking and was glad to have something to take his visitors' minds off the meal. After the initial excitement, it wasn't long before the cold night forced them into their bunks.

The Tundra Buggy is heavy with the smell of sleeping bodies. Chuck Ford lies awake, swigging bourbon from his sliver flask. This cold, bare room filled with the mutterings of male dreams takes him back to his father's house in the Bitterroot Mountains of Montana. There, his father had always felt like an immigrant, a displaced person. Displaced out of his home state of Alaska by the Alaska Pipeline. They had bought him out. He hadn't wanted to sell. Spent everything he had fighting to keep what he and his father had built. When he understood that he had no rights, no right to his family home, he left. Took his wife and young sons into a Rocky Mountain wilderness from which he preached the democracy of complete and utter self-sufficiency. Allegiance was to mother earth, not mother land. The only flag he saluted, and he said this without humor, was the raised tail of a fleeing whitetail deer. He had lived long enough to know that his eldest son was waging a holy war.

To the darkness Charles Wiseman Ford the Third speaks, "Don't worry, Daddy, Churchill ain't that far from Juneau, just you wait and see." He salutes—the silver of his flask ghosting to white in the single exit light over the door. "You know, old man, I had a sign. This place in Canada, this Churchill is 58° N and Juneau is 58° N . . . sitting right there on that same line like frozen dog turds. The greater part of a country apart, but that's nothing in the scheme of things, just you wait and see."

CAPE CHURCHILL
November 1, 1986

CONRAD BUZZES THE CAMP, then sets the Jet Ranger down in front of the tower. He looks up to see Guy racing toward the helicopter.

Guy ducks under the rotors, yanks open Conrad's door and shouts above the noise, "Chuck's missing. Need you to go up and have a look."

Conrad gives him the thumbs up, pulls his door shut and, in short order, Conrad, Allsun and Neal are in the air again.

They're attracted to a patch of Ungava willow by milling scavengers.

THE RCMP OFFICER arrives by Twin Otter from Churchill around noon. The pilot of the fixed-wing sets the balloon tires down on a gravel beach that serves as a landing strip. A grim party watches from the tower.

Guy descends the ladder to escort the Mountie and the Calmair pilot across the open area. Jud follows him down to the lab trailer, where he reappears in the roof hatch with a shotgun. Hal, Pete and Lucas stare down at the scrub willow by the pothole lake.

Allsun and Neal expect they will all be summoned, one by one, down to the Tundra Buggy to be interviewed. To their surprise, the officer starts up the tower ladder to the hut.

Guy introduces Constable Klassen. To Conrad, she's Karen.

Would you like a cup of tea and a bannock sandwich?" Guy offers.

The pilot nods.

"No, thanks." Constable Klassen takes a good look at what they're eating—peanut butter and jam between two slabs of Guy's famous skillet-baked bread. She examines the room as she takes out her notebook and pencil. "Mr. Thorpe, could you tell me when and where you last saw Mr. Ford?"

"After supper we did a bit of socializing up here."

"Alcohol was involved?" The constable makes quick notes in shorthand.

"We each had a couple shots of brandy. Chuck had his own supply of bourbon." Guy's voice is neutral.

"How much would you say he had to drink?" Cst. Klassen's focus is Guy, but she is also aware of how the others in the cramped room are responding to her questions.

"Don't know. Not for sure. But he knew, just like I knew, that he'd have to get down the tower ladder." Guy wonders if she's intimating that he runs a slack operation.

"You don't sleep up here?" Cst. Klassen nods at the bunks.

"Well, yeah, Jud and I, not Chuck. He was bunking in

the Tundra Buggy." Guy is getting restive with this line of inquiry.

"So, in your estimation, Mr. Ford had between one and three ounces of whiskey?" The young constable wants details, some measure of exactitude in the messy business of living . . . and dying.

"I don't—"

Pete speaks up. "Chuck had a flask going in the Tundra Buggy."

Cst. Klassen takes in the man with the ripped jacket. "And you are?"

"Pete. Chuck's cameraman, Pete Paul."

"Alright, Mr. Paul, just when was this?" The constable looks up from her notebook to make eye contact.

"When we went to bed. He . . . Chuck doesn't sleep too good, so he'd have a few to help him nod off. Pretty much all the time, eh?" Pete looks to Lucas but not Hal for affirmation.

"What time would you say this was, Mr. Paul?" Cst. Klassen holds his gaze so he doesn't look to his friend for collaboration.

"Geez, maybe eleven o'clock, around there. We watched the northern lights for a while from the Buggy deck . . . but we got cold pretty fast."

The officer directs her attention to the friend. "So, you were all in bed by what time, Mr. . . . ?"

"Clark, Lucas Clark, Ma'am. By eleven. Don't spend much time outside your sleeping bag in that Tundra bunkhouse. Freeze the nuts off a bridge."

Cst. Klassen gives him a careful look, then turns to the others for names and details.

She surveys her notes, and turns back to Guy. "Mr.

Thorpe, you and Mr. Ash spent the night up here, is that right?"

"Yes, we sleep up here."

"What time did you turn in?" she asks.

"About the same time as the others, around eleven, I guess. Came up from watching the northern lights and talked to Conrad on the radio."

"And you, Mr. Ash. You were here at that time?"

"No, I went to the lab trailer to finish up some work." Jud remains perfectly still, perfectly contained. Everything about him is neutral, especially his moon face.

"How long were you there?" Cst. Klassen notes his lack of animation.

"Couple of hours."

"And then?"

"I packed it in and came up to bed."

"Can you give me an approximation on the time? One, two o'clock?"

"Two, two thirty."

"Mr. Thorpe, did you hear or see Mr. Ash enter this room in the early hours of the morning?" The officer keeps her eyes on Jud while asking this question of Guy.

"No. I would have been asleep by then."

"And Mr. Ash, did you see or hear anything unusual while you were working?"

"Didn't hear anything unusual. Can't see out of the lab trailer."

Cst. Klassen reads through her notes, makes some additions. Those assembled wait in silence.

She directs her attention to Guy. "You said on the radio, you brought the body back. I'd like to see it."

"It's not really a body. That is ..." Guy falters.

"Karen, you know what bears can do," Conrad speaks as one local to another. "We brought back what was left. The bag's in the storage cage ... frozen."

"I'd like to go out to the discovery site as well." She closes her notebook.

"I can take you in the chopper."

"Thanks, Conrad, but I'd like to walk it." She catches the look on Guy's face. "Is that a problem?"

"We can provide protection," Guy says, "but I would prefer you went by helicopter."

"I want those who found the body to accompany me and Mr. Thorpe." Cst. Klassen zips up her standard midnight blue parka and flips the hood up over her government-issue beaver hat with earflaps tied neatly on top.

Guy leaves Jud and Chuck's crew to watch for bears. Jud is to signal those on the ground with a flare, if bears approach the camp or the search party.

BEYOND THE BAIT site the cautious searchers find and follow a crystalline trail of red across skiff snow and rocks. Where they enter the scrub willow fringing the small lake, they notice broken twigs and a more obvious drag trail than they could see on the frozen tundra. Cst. Klassen photographs bits of cloth caught on the brittle willow wands. She takes notes despite the below-zero temperature and gets shots of the trail every couple of feet.

The investigation progresses slowly. She is very thorough. Perhaps it's because she's young and doesn't want to make a mistake, although she seems confident enough in her authority.

Preoccupied with the difficulty of shooting blood splattered on gravel and the chore of adjusting her camera, the constable doesn't seem to notice the bears zeroing in on the willow bluff. Knowledge of the kill site and human activity there has had the same effect on the polar bears as the lighted bait barbecue does.

At the spot where Chuck's remains were found, Guy interrupts as the officer examines the site and fires questions at Neal and Conrad. "Constable Klassen," Guy says with urgency, "we have to get back to camp, now." He points to a rise above the pothole lake: a mother and two yearlings are approaching from the north, and from the east, three females or subadult males are closing in fast.

"Just a minute." She waves Guy off. Something has caught her eye in a section of trampled twigs. The constable shifts a silver object with her pencil, then takes two quick pictures.

"Now!" Guy shouts, his single command punctuated by the hiss of a flare shot from the tower.

Constable Klassen grabs up Chuck's flattened silver flask and makes a dash for camp with the others. Bears do not usually run down prey, but the invitation to chase is a strong, instinctive response.

The search party hustles across the esker as if part of some fantastical parade complete with fireworks. The first few Crackers and Bangers slow the bears, but, for the most part, they ignore the noisy birds made of fire and light.

Then the unexpected happens: a bear comes toward them from the camp.

"Neal!" Guy shouts.

Neal's attention is focused behind the group. He turns, spots the big male bear, adjusts his position, raising the 38-mm single shot to his shoulder, and fires. A black rubber bullet hits the polar bear square in the chest. It will have less impact there, but it's the best angle Neal had. He reloads.

The bear stumbles, snaps its jaws and keeps coming. From the tower, Jud launches a Cracker Shell low, causing the male to raise its head, and Neal fires again. This rubber bullet is right on target: the left front shoulder near the top of the back.

To their amazement, the big male continues the charge unfazed. Constable Klassen has drawn her side arm. She takes a two-handed stance.

The group comes together in a tight circle like defensive musk oxen. Allsun shouts at the advancing bear, loud angry words. The others join in.

Sprinting the distance, the great white bear streamlines into a long, low stretch, charging within ten yards. Then suddenly it veers away from this bristling, noisy herd.

The way is clear to the tower. In deference to the big male, the bears behind them don't follow.

Back at the tower, Constable Klassen doesn't refuse the offer of a cup of tea this time. Once they all stop trembling, ostensibly from the cold, the young constable asks for an escort to the plane. She leaves with the dark green bags from the storage cage and no doubts about bear activity at the Cape.

FROM INSIDE THE Tundra Buggy, they hear the Twin Otter climb, circle and retreat toward Churchill. They seem to be holding their collective breath. Air fills the void within and without. There is much to say; not one of them knows how to begin. The moment holds their mortality up, suspended on tension and recognition.

Conrad notices Hal staring at Chuck's bunk. No one had sat there. The yellow sleeping bag gapes open. Chuck's gear is back under the plywood bunk. The Mountie had looked through it before she left.

"I'll take you back to Churchill, if you like," Conrad says to Hal.

"Yes . . . I think," Hal looks at Pete and Lucas, "I think we need to get out of here."

"Half an hour?"

"Yeah, that's good. We'll be ready."

Conrad follows Allsun out of the Tundra Buggy. Guy, Neal and Jud are on the tower platform, crossing to the lab trailer.

"Come back to Churchill with me," Conrad says to Allsun. "I can bring you out here tomorrow morning."

Allsun watches the retreating backs of the men. "I should stay and keep an eye on Neal . . . at least until the test results come back."

Conrad is standing behind Allsun. "Guy's here." He is trying to sound practical, not insistent.

"Conrad, I think maybe it's me that needs watching." She cannot turn to face him.

"What do you mean? Are you ill? Maybe we should—"

Allsun shivers. "Let's go up the tower and have some tea."

Conrad notices that Allsun climbs the tower ladder with

swift assurance. If she's ill, it's not a sickness of the body.

The heater in the hut had been turned off and the small room has cooled down. Allsun removes only her mitts to light the Coleman stove and put the kettle on. She gladly leaves the lighting of the propane heater to Conrad. He waits for her to speak.

Allsun fusses with the tea, while she tries to find words for what she feels. "Conrad, I don't know what last night was about."

"About?" Conrad rises to look at her, the burning match still in his fingers. He shakes out the flame.

"I don't want you to be ... an escape. That wouldn't be fair." The tremendous release she had felt—was that from loneliness, from lust, from a million other negatives that crowd her life? In his face she wants desperately to see the answers.

"Fair for who? You? Me? We connected. It's that simple ... at least it is for me." He would like to hold her, to reassure her, but he senses she feels cornered. Not the time to approach.

"But you know my situation?" She looks away, behind him to the door and beyond. And she reminds herself, it's just going to get more complicated once she gets home.

"Yes, but that doesn't change how I feel about you. It's strong, Allsun. I haven't felt this way in a long time." Can she hear how deep these words run?

"That's what scares me. There's no room in my life for ... there's Damon and ... it's not possible."

"I don't believe that. What I do know is you have some decisions to make." He turns momentarily in the direction of her gaze.

"What?" Is he throwing down some kind of ultimatum? Who does he think he is? One night doesn't mean—

Conrad reads the thoughts flashing like wildfire across her face. "I can wait, that's all I'm saying."

Conrad closes the door behind him.

Allsun stands in the middle of the little room. Minutes later the door flies open. There's no one there. She has the wind for a companion.

GUY OPENS A couple of cans of chicken noodle soup and fries up some bannock. Supper is a listless, quiet affair.

Allsun makes yet another pot of tea, but this time she spikes it with a shot of Southern Comfort from a bottle she keeps in her pack. She considers The Grand Old Drink of the South a painkiller. One in a long line selected in response to what is on the outside of the bottle, not the inside. Allsun likes the pictures and chooses her tipple accordingly. The drawing on the label of the Southern Comfort bottle could have been done by Krieghoff, on vacation in the deep south with its plantation homes and steamboats. The history on the back of the bottle verifies her supposition: "Over a century ago in the city of New Orleans, where the Mississippi River flows out of the heartland of America, a smooth, full-bodied spirit was born. Through the era of the great Mississippi River steamboats and the birth of American Jazz and Blues, Southern Comfort became The Grand Old Drink of the South." In 1870 Cornelius David Krieghoff would have been fifty-five and conceivably sick and tired of rendering snow-filled winter scenes of Quebec. Yes, it would have been time for him to sit on some shaded verandah and swap stories with Audubon's ghost.

Replacing the cap on the bottle, Allsun's flight of fancy is brought up short by another ghost—Chuck Ford was from New Orleans. Does he have a family there? Who will tell them?

Allsun hands around mugs of tea. The steam is fragrant with the smell of ripe fruit. She hears Jud say, "Bears will kill sled dogs—"

"And befriend them," Neal counters, as he fishes his mouth organ from his pocket. "Right, Al?"

"What?" She's still looking for some comfort in her tea cup.

"You know, those incredible pictures you showed me." Neal blows the pocket lint out of the reeds.

"The shots by Norbert Rosing, is that what you're talking about?"

He nods, blows a few clean single notes.

"God, he lucked out." She sips her brew. "To be there when a polar bear and a staked-out sled dog decide to play together. I mean, just the fact that the dog is tethered ...it's like having them in his studio. And for a whole ten days. Incredible." The liqueur-laced tea expands the room. Allsun exhales and the walls inflate. For an aberrant moment she feels as though she's inside a lung.

"Perhaps the bear had a man's spirit for those days," Guy says, more to himself than to the others.

Neal stops tonguing his harmonica and exchanges a look with Allsun.

"What do you know of bear spirits?" Neal asks from the bunk where he's stretched out.

"Oh, what I've been told, mostly." Guy gives them a tentative glance.

"Such as?" Neal persists.

"There's lots of native stories, of course," he begins. "The Inuit have been living with the bears for more than a thousand years. They see them differently. It's like day-to-day stuff . . . the things you know inside out, down to the smallest detail . . . in this way even objects become an integral part of your life. We watch with more than our eyes, we humans."

Neal goes back to warming up his harp. He's not about to discuss northern mysticism with Guy. He considers it Guy's way of reconciling Jane's death and he wants no part of it.

Allsun cannot leave Guy hanging out there. "I read Rasmussen's *Eskimo Folk Tales* before I came up here," she says. "What I found curious about the Inuit legends is the belief that polar bears are people in fur coats. For egocentric humans, that's a pretty big leap." She smiles, hoping to break the tension with an innocuous observation.

"Based on similarities." Guy returns her smile. "The polar bears hunt and eat the same foods as the people of the seal—"

"Including the people of the seal." Jud enters the conversation for the first time since wrapping both hands around his tea mug.

"Polar bears hunt men, which puts them on a much more even footing." Guy's pronouncement elicits silence.

The others watch as he kneels beside his bunk. Allsun thinks, "Now I lay me down to sleep, I pray the Lord my soul to keep." Guy pulls a hockey bag from under the bed.

Jud has long since registered the tension among the three friends and decides to give the conversation a push to see where it will go. "It's a powerful animal in its own right."

"Yes, and who wouldn't want to associate with that power?" Guy stares out past his own reflection in the darkened window. "The great shaman took the polar bear as a spiritual guardian." Despite what he perceives as Neal's hostile indifference, he will not be silenced. But the North has taught him patience. Now is not the time to hold up his new way of thinking for Neal to examine and perhaps dismiss. He draws a scratched and bruised six-string guitar from his hockey bag.

Neal studies Guy as he sits in the wooden chair tuning the guitar. "The Inuit in the Beaufort hunted down the bear that killed our rig worker—"

"Old stories," Allsun utters abruptly. She is tired of their attempts to draw new scars on an old wound. "Native stories about people visiting homes where they thought humans lived only to discover their hosts were human-like because they took off their fur coats once inside. Or the bear who was attacked by sled dogs and with one swipe of his paw turned the dogs into the stars that form the constellation Qilugtussat . . . it looks like barking dogs surrounding a bear." Her voice is hard, obstinate—these are the stories she wants to hear, stories full of wonder, not grief and grievance.

Jud sits back on his bunk. His face remains in the shadows beyond the single lamp. "'The greatest peril of life lies in the fact that human food consists entirely of souls.

All the creatures that we have to kill and eat, all those that we have to strike down and destroy to make clothes for ourselves, have souls, like we have, souls that do not perish with the body, and which must therefore be propitiated lest they should avenge themselves on us for taking away their bodies.'" He is quoting from the Danish ethnologist Knud Rasmussen's interview with Ivaluardjuk, an Igloolik Inuk hunter. He could be talking in his sleep: like the words, his voice sounds as if it belongs to someone else.

While Jud spoke, Guy had stopped tuning the old Martin six-string. He now tests the guitar's sound with a few blues licks. He plays an opening riff.

"What key are you in?" Neal asks.

"Blow me a note and I'll tune to you."

"Okay." Neal raises the harp to his lips.

Guy cocks his head to listen. In the white gas shadows he reminds Allsun of the tame crow her sister trained to speak.

"Alright, E it is," Guy confirms. "Neal, do you remember Robert Johnson?"

"Do I remember Robert Johnson? Does a bear shit in the woods?" As quickly as he had become sullen, Neal brightens.

"Damn right." There is relief in Guy's voice. "I've collected a truck load." Guy grins at Neal.

"Are we talkin' scats or scats?" Neal grins right back.

Allsun groans, recognizing they're warming up more than their instruments. At university, the three bears would take a pun over a pint any day.

"We talkin' 'The Curse-ed Ursid Blues.' " Guy has added a little down-home flavor to his speech.

"Shit?" Neal renders a call of sorts on his harmonica, a rude sound. "What tune is that to? I don't remember."

"Mr. Johnson's famous 'Malted Milk.'"

"Yeah, that's it. Okay, I got it, let's go." Neal raises the harp to his mouth.

"One, two, three ..." Guy launches into the lyrics:

The Bear is classed a car-ni-vore
    the world has eight fine species
But classifyin' their foods is tough
    we're forced to study feces
I got the pain-in-the-Ursus blues
I got the pain-in-the-Ursus blues
    Y'all can see it on my shoes

I tried to study English
    took astrophysics theories
But found they was just relative
    and so made other queries
I got the pain-in-the-Ursus blues
I got the pain-in-the-Ursus blues
    from payin' the grad school dues

So now I study Ursids
    those Miocene descendants
Adaptive opportunists
    they're promiscuous contestants
I got the pain-in-the-Ursus blues
I got the pain-in-the-Ursus blues
    it's the path I chose to choose

Now convocation's imminent
I know the history of the species
the feces in my thesis
and my funding's history too
I tried to dump the feelin'
But I still got them curse-ed Ursid blues

The song is as slow as a dream. Neal is beating out the time, getting a feel for the chord progressions and the rhythm. He slides in gently with a four draw, holds it for a couple of beats, does some tonguing to add feeling. He's playing Cross Harp, bending notes, waiting, putting the grit in his blues harmonica.

Guy stops singing and nods as Neal works some riffs, building tension to the point where Guy comes in with the last chorus,

I got the pain-in-the-Ursus blues
I got the pain-in-the-Ursus blues
I tried to duuump the feelin'
But I still got them curs-ed Ursid blues

Guy ends with a guitar flourish.

"What was *that* bit of business, Guy?" Allsun asks, trying hard to keep a straight face.

Guy recognizes the smirk behind her question. "It's what the boys in the band call 'masturbating.' "

"An apt musical term," she replies.

" 'Kind Hearted Woman' . . ." Neal says.

"Well, thankya, sir," Allsun quips.

Guy is struggling to tune his guitar, made recalcitrant by the meat-locker temperature of the hut. " 'Kind Hearted

Woman Blues' it is. Mr. Johnson, we ask your indulgence."

As Guy and Neal find their way back to Hazelhurst, Mississippi, Jud rolls up his sleeping bag, stuffs it in his backpack and makes for the door.

Guy looks up. "You turning in?" he asks with some surprise. "Check the furnace in the Tundra Buggy before you settle in."

"Yeah," is all Jud offers, and he's gone.

"Didn't think our playin' was that bad," Guy says. "He's never in bed before midnight or later."

"It's been a hell of a day." Neal drops his hands and the harmonica into his lap. His face is drawn, bone white in the white gas light.

An image of Neal lying on the Tundra Buggy deck causes Allsun to examine the scabs on the undersides of her fingers. "How you feeling?" she asks him.

"Wiped."

"Maybe we should call it a day," Guy suggests. "I'll bunk in the Tundra Buggy. You two can stay up here if you like."

"You're not going make us get back on the horse? What kind of psychology is that?" Neal gives Guy a wry smile.

"Jud talks in his sleep," Guy explains, recognizing that Neal does not want him to caretake.

"That must be interesting."

"Creepy is more like it. Gotta be nightmares he's having." Guy frowns.

"He seems an odd one." Allsun reads Guy's perplexed look.

"Don't know much about him, really. Works hard. Tell you, though, I always get the feeling with Jud he's watching and waiting."

"It's what we do out here ... watch and wait." Neal is off-handed.

"For bears. Jud's waiting for something else." Guy shakes his head as if to clear his vision.

"Like what?" Allsun asks.

"I have no idea. Just sense it."

"Well, I got the feeling he knew Chuck," Allsun says to Guy. She wonders if this is what he's picking up on.

"From television." Neal is dismissive. "Probably grew up on *Wild World*. Chuck Ford's the reason he's taking biology!"

"He doesn't strike me as the fan type. A loner for sure, with a trap door I'm not convinced I'd want to fall through." Guy stares at what had been Jud's bunk.

"Speaking of doors," Allsun has just remembered, "talking to Richard Rowan last night in Churchill, he said there was ice on the latch in the observation cage. Does that happen as a rule?"

Guy had risen to put his guitar away; he stops to look at her. "Ice on the latch? Shouldn't be ice on the latch."

"I was wondering if that had something to do with it giving way?" Allsun watches Guy's eyebrows rise and the familiar lines in his forehead deepen.

"What's this?" Neal asks.

Both Guy and Allsun turn to Neal. "Yesterday," Allsun fills him in, "Richard Rowan was shooting from the observation cage. Taking a pounding when the latch broke and the door flew open."

"Holy shit! What happened?" Neal can't believe he hadn't been told.

Guy sits back down in the chair, his guitar forgotten. "A fucking waste, that's what happened," he says with such venom, he paralyzes words of response. Guy is perfectly still, except for his eyes. He is reviewing the events. "You know, I thought the latch might have been damaged when Jud and Chuck moved the cage. But I don't understand how moisture would get on it. They dragged it across freeze-dried tundra, for Christ's sake."

"You know what I think?" Neal's eyes are dark with anger. "I think we better watch our backs. There's been too many so-called accidents out here."

Allsun and Guy are astounded.

"Are you serious?" Guy manages.

"But who—"

"Who knows? This place has been a circus in the last few days . . . people in and out, wanting different things from being here." Neal is determined to have them see what he has suddenly seen. It's the third man on the match—his grandfather telling him that it wasn't a matter of bad luck that the third soldier to light his cigarette off a single match didn't get a chance to inhale. Time enough for the flame and the man to become a target. Three serious events, three targets; who is on the firing line? "We need to think about it."

"Geez, Neal, I can't get my head around that!" Guy has started to pace, carrying his guitar by the neck like a club.

"Look, this place is going turn into the big top again tomorrow with Suzuki and the CBC crew coming in—"

Guy wheels on Allsun. "Is Rowan coming back?"

"I don't know. You'll have to give Conrad a call on that," Allsun says, her voice calm, rational. She'd like Guy to stop pacing so she can focus on thinking through the implications of what Neal has conjured.

"Will Rowan be at Conrad's?" Guy asks.

"No." Allsun is confused. "He's staying at the Inn."

"But didn't you both stay at Conrad's last night?" Guy has put down his guitar in favor of the radio microphone.

"No. Like I said, Richard is staying at the Arctic Inn." Allsun's tone makes it clear there is nothing more to say.

GUY HAS LEFT Allsun and Neal to bunk in the tower hut, while he joins the restive Jud in the Tundra Buggy. A waning moon cuts a path through the night, lasering the window above Allsun's head.

Neal speaks from the bunk in the long shadows below the other window. "Not what I had in mind for you."

"Sorry?"

"Thought being here would give us a chance to get away and talk." Despite the smallness of the room, Neal sounds distant. Night and shadow have a way of changing perspective. "I wanted to tell you I'm over Jane. I'm ready to move on."

Tension, the hint of something unsaid, raises the hairs on the back of Allsun's neck. "I'm happy for you, Neal. I know it hasn't been easy."

"For either of us. I often think about what we've gone through . . . you and I. How much our lives have been twisted by misery and grief. We deserve better, you know." His voice is barely above a whisper, but still full of conviction.

Allsun recognizes his tone as the same one she uses to control a skittish horse. "I make my own choices, that way I'm not owed anything by the world." She will not be led.

"I've always admired your strength. But you don't have to go it alone." Neal is conciliatory.

The moon has risen higher in the sky, angling pale light onto Neal's face. He lies on his back, his face half dark and half light. "Neal, what are you saying?" Allsun wants whatever is at the bottom of this conversation out in the open.

"You," he says quietly. "I want you."

"We're friends." Allsun knows this isn't about friendship.

"Yes, we have a history. All the better—"

"I have Damon."

"We have Damon. We share your—"

"No, we don't share Damon. He's my husband, your friend ... our love, our grief, yours and mine are different." Her feelings are the one single thing she owns. There is no one who can lay claim to them.

"Al, don't shut me out." Neal's words are more angry than anguished. "I heard what Guy said. You stayed with Conrad last night. How can—"

"Drop it, Neal. You're my friend, not my keeper." Lying there in silence, Allsun is amazed at the rage that washes over her. In her mind, she sees a photograph of her face disappear in a bleach bath.

"I can be more. I want you to know that." Neal sounds resigned.

Allsun doesn't trust herself to speak.

CAPE CHURCHILL
November 2, 1986

CONRAD HAS BARELY UNLOADED David Suzuki and *The Nature of Things* crew when the CBC producer is asking about Chuck Ford's death. The news is definitely out there in the wide world.

Guy's offer of a safety tour is taken up immediately. There is nothing reticent about the response. David Suzuki suggests the crew film the tour. A canny idea that none of the other media had been shrewd enough to hatch. This allows Suzuki, as host, to introduce the location in a dynamic fashion—no wasted footage here. He questions each step of the safety procedure, eliciting scientific information and anecdotal stories from Guy and Neal.

Allsun takes her lead from Suzuki and becomes part of the filming entourage. She shoots the Canadian Broadcasting Company shooting the camp's safety protocol, which gives her a series of camp shots that include the highly recognizable face of one of Canada's passionate nature advocates.

On the way back to the Tundra Buggy, Guy stops beside the lab trailer. He invites Suzuki to get down on all fours and join him under the trailer. Those toting cameras are not sure they like this bit of business, until Guy tells his guest that they are curled up where, nightly, polar bears lie in wait. It will make for good copy.

Down on all fours, an undignified shooting position, Allsun hears the roof hatch to the lab trailer open. Jud hoists himself out to see what's going on. He must have heard Guy and David through the trailer floor. Does he hear the bears at night when he's working? What does he hear? Polar bears are not particularly vocal, especially if they're stalking. Quiet is measurable here. Can he hear them breathe?

Allsun rises up, gets him in her sights and in rapid succession knocks off a number of shots. He disappears down the hatch as if it's a bolt-hole.

THE TUNDRA BUGGY is again overcrowded, if not overheated. Allsun notices that not only are the few windows rimed with frost, but also the ceiling has a thin slick of frozen condensation. All their hot air rising and meeting a metallic-blue cold front. With the *Wild World* crew gone, Pete can't blame the American presence. Richard Rowan, the lone representative from south of the border, has cornered David Suzuki, holding him with contentious conversation.

Jud had been surprised to see Richard Rowan get out of the helicopter when it arrived at camp that morning. After Rowan's bear scare in the observation cage, he figured this troublesome journalist was long gone. Although Jud got the impression Ford wouldn't have minded something more permanent, Chuck was pleased with

Rowan's departure. Ford considered Richard Rowan a threat to LIB. Of course, he hadn't shared with Jud what kind of threat. Just another example of Ford's diminishing abilities—treating him like a lackey instead of a LIB soldier. Jud wonders why Rowan is back, now Ford is gone. Has he come back for him?

Guy is in another corner with Conrad, finalizing the afternoon survey of the polar bear maternity dens at Owl River. They agree this is probably their last chance before the weather comes in and shuts the research program down. Conrad confirms the storm warning Guy received over the radio at 6:00 a.m.—blizzard conditions by tomorrow afternoon.

Neal has started out on the path of least resistance in the form of small talk with the CBC producer and his soundman. But the producer, Gord Kingston, has an agenda: spooked by Chuck's death, which he learned about from several national newspapers on the plane coming north, Gord wants reassurance that today's filming will be accident free. With this turn in the conversation, Neal beckons Guy over, and Allsun gives up her seat on the bunk, moving across to the bed that had been Chuck's. Guy pulls Suzuki and Rowan into the discussion as he outlines the procedures for the deterrence testing they're about to film.

The first question comes from Richard Rowan. "So, where's the best position to shoot the bear spray test?"

"Depends on wind direction. You don't want this on your camera equipment. There's an orange dye in it." Neal is trying to decide how much to tell them about this new deterrent without giving them a lecture in better living through chemistry.

"Bugger the equipment. What about my eyes?" *Bugger?* For an American, Richard certainly has a command of the Queen's English.

"Goes without saying." Neal glances at Allsun, wanting to keep her nearby, hoping she'll stay, although she knows all about the bear spray. He had filled a good hour of their flight out from Calgary with his plans for this new safety device. "Painful."

"Very." Guy adds his own admonition. "High on the pain scale. Used in medical research—"

"Administered to get peripheral pain receptors to fire. It was successful in the extreme." Neal is quick to elaborate.

"You're telling me bear spray is used in medical research?" Richard looks from one to the other.

"No, bear spray is the result of pain research." Neal corrects this misrepresentation. "More specifically, capsaicin, the active ingredient derived from red peppers." He watches as Suzuki makes notes. Neal decides to lighten things up. "A taste of Mexico for zeees bruto blanco. Habanero peppers es óptimo."

"I see you speak my country's unofficial second language. Bien?" Richard is so droll that the only remedy is to laugh at him. He takes it well, seeming pleased they got his clever reference to their French Canadian heritage.

"Ne vous en faites pas! No problemo!" Neal adds, to Richard's confusion. "The bear spray has a range of six meters ... twenty feet. Close up and personal. Since I can't use the observation cage, I'll be in the storage cage. So, you're going to have to shoot from the deck of the Tundra Buggy. Well out of range of the spray."

"It's going to be tight," Guy assures them.

"Is the stuff good? Does it work?" Richard appears to have accepted the shooting arrangements.

"Aggressive grizzlies, 94 percent; aggressive black bears, 100 percent in limited test numbers. But there's lots for consideration: the wind, the cold, both affect delivery; you've got to spray it right in the bear's face, essentially at close range; if you've got a starving bear, you've got a determined bear. Testing here is the ultimate challenge for the product." Neal hears the flipping of notebook pages. His attention is on Allsun as she rises and moves to the outside of the group gathered around him.

"So, when you spray these poor, unsuspecting polar bears, what will actually happen to them?" Richard takes her place on the bunk.

"The spray irritates their eyes, nose and respiratory tract. It lasts as little as five minutes and at most fifteen. You've got to be fast if you're in the wild. Get out of the situation while you've still got some bear spray left in the canister. Shouldn't have to shoot your whole wad at once." Neal watches—Allsun at the edge looking a little lost.

"And no lasting side effects?" Richard quizzes.

Neal knows how sensitive a question this is. "Well," he pauses, "an aversion to Mexican food. But only observed in dump bears."

Richard gives Neal a hard look, then joins in the laughter.

Cut loose, Allsun heads for Pierre La Croix, the CBC cameraman. He's standing at the counter checking over his equipment.

"May I?" She reaches for the small folding knife lying beside his gear on the counter top.

"Yeah, sure." Pierre glances at her with interest.

Allsun opens out the blade to find an exquisite piece of Damascus steel, its surface an hallucination of swirls. "Whoa, that's one fancy folder."

He nods.

"That machined handle ...bit of camouflage for what's inside. I like the idea." She judges the knife's overall length to be a bit more than eight inches.

"Got tired of getting ripped off," is Pierre's reply.

For a moment she's at a loss.

"Anything looks like an art knife . . . shoosh, gone. When I worked in Montreal, three knives gone, just like that. Big money." Pierre shakes his head in agreement with his memory.

"Montrealers! Art lovers!" Allsun is the recipient of a stare that questions her sincerity, so she moves on quickly. "It's pretty light. This handle's gotta be titanium? That ain't cheap." She is struck by the double contradiction: an expensive folding knife, the handle plain enough to go unremarked; and the juxtaposition of old and new, Damascus steel and titanium.

His complete attention is on her for the first time. "How do you know knives?"

"The way I know most things these days. I've written about them. Covered an international knife show last year in Frankfurt." She thinks Pierre had been looking for more from her. "Neal," Allsun points to the bunk behind them, "came along to Germany as my resident expert."

Pierre glances back.

"Neal got interested when he was a kid. First knife he made . . . a big, ugly hunting knife with a deer antler handle . . . and a blade made from an old car spring. Hell, the filing that went into that thing! His mom told me it kept him out of trouble for nearly a year."

Taking another look at Neal, the cameraman smiles knowingly.

"A lot of culture wrapped up in those knives," Allsun says to Pierre.

He regards her with a quizzical look that ever so slightly raises his thick, black eyebrows. The taciturn side of his Gaulish inheritance.

"The Frankfurt show . . . a history lesson, really. I got a sense of this going between displays, taking photographs. But it wasn't until I was checking the contact sheets without my shot list that I realized the knives not only had personality, they had nationality. Knives from Brazil, Russia, Italy, Canada—they all may be made of the same steel, bone, ivory, mother-of-pearl, but the designs belong to the place. Canada and Brazil, psyches and knives forged out of frontier experiences, you know, hunters and skinners. While, say, Russia and Italy, the Europeans are making high art, have been for centuries." The taciturn Pierre brings out the talker in Allsun.

Pierre examines his knife, the streamline of steel into titanium. "Yes," he says, as he folds the mosaic blade into the NASA handle. "The past is a sharp blade hiding in a deceptive present."

Allsun is speechless. She finally chides Pierre, "Where were you when I was writing that article?"

He acknowledges the compliment with a genuine smile.

History, Allsun thinks. She and Neal in Frankfurt—a city remade around a bombed-out shell of history. She had been glad to leave; the city was too much like her. Neal had wanted to stay on after the knife show, but when she said she was going home, he came away with her. Had Neal been trying to give them a history that didn't include Damon? After Neal's bombshell last night, she isn't sure how he has been viewing these last four years of their friendship. Had he written Damon off from the start? That wasn't possible; Neal and Damon had been like brothers. The past is a sharp blade hiding in a deceptive present.

THE CBC FILMING of the regular deterrence testing goes off without a hitch. The first wave of bears has been chased to the outskirts of camp, and the *Nature of Things* crew, Richard Rowan and Allsun are quickly repositioning to shoot the Bear Spray test. Richard climbs onto the roof of the Tundra Buggy to relieve the crowding on the Buggy deck.

Neal waits in the storage cage ready for the ambush, armed with three 290-gram metal canisters that would have the innocuous appearance of whipped cream dispensers, were it not for the gun-like grip of the handles. Neal thinks that, as handles go, it's not a bad design: heavy black plastic with a bright yellow trigger integral to the top of the grip, except for a safety device that looks like the pull-pin of a hand grenade. In the shape of a small *q*, the thin metal tail fits into a slot in the handle below the trigger to stop it from being depressed unintentionally. But this safety feature keeps falling out, to Neal's dismay.

He's fiddling with the pull-pin on a can of bear spray called Animal Attack Repellent, when a young male bear appears behind the storage cage. Neal remains still, allowing the polar bear to explore the area and gradually come into range. When the bear crosses the line, the six-meter-line Neal has squeezed onto the snow from a plastic bottle of hair dye, the white bear is met with a blast full in the face. He shakes his head and scuttles to the side. But the spray is a meter wide, there is no relief to the side. The bear turns, runs, then dives head-first into the snow, rolling and rubbing its head. The researchers note this as interesting behavior, although polar bears are known to roll around giving themselves snow baths. The capsaicin and the orange dye remain. The photographers are enthralled.

Another bear has found Neal. This one is no adolescent. It is fully grown and one of the largest the camp has seen. The size, the broadness of the skull, the black scars on the face define this bear as undeniably male. He's not marked, which means he's most likely a newcomer.

Agitated, perhaps by what remains of the pepper spray in the air, he trots toward the cage. His head is low in threat posture. Inside the six-meter mark, he issues a loud, open-mouthed hiss. Neal shoots from a new canister. Sonic quick, the bear rises onto his hind legs, hitting the cage with a boom. Neal sprays two long bursts. The bear continues to pound the cage, making it rock, even though it is anchored by heavy fuel drums and other materials piled on the floor.

Allsun is cranking off shots, holding her breath the way she does when she shoots.

She hears Pierre gasp. He has been filming beside her. His chest heaves, trying to pull air into his lungs. His gloved hands are at his eyes.

Allsun slams open the door of the Tundra Buggy, pushes Pierre through. She's behind him, David Suzuki on her heels. Pierre falls onto a bunk. Allsun scoops water from a pail to flush his eyes, while David unzips Pierre's jacket.

"AR," Allsun says to Suzuki. Trying not to shout, trying to stay calm for Pierre. "He can't breathe." She can think of nothing other than artificial respiration.

Pierre is losing consciousness as David rolls him from his side onto his back, straightening his legs from the fetal position he had taken on the bunk.

Allsun pulls off her jacket and folds it under Pierre's shoulders, tilting his head back.

David is on his knees, one hand under Pierre's chin. He takes a deep breath, covers Pierre's mouth with his own, and pinches the cameraman's nose shut with the fingers of his free hand. He blows into Pierre's lungs; his chest rises. He removes his mouth, counts the seconds, inhales and repeats the cycle.

Allsun stands by, ready to spell David off. She's trembling. For a moment she is back again on the Tundra Buggy deck and Neal is lying at her feet.

Pierre's eyes start to flutter. He's regaining consciousness. Suddenly his eyes twitch open, focusing on David giving him the kiss of life.

Suzuki straightens from this embrace. Pierre is breathing on his own, not without difficulty. When he finds enough air, he asks, "Who's at the camera?"

"Gord took over," David says smiling. "How you doing?"

Pierre nods.

"You gave us quite a scare," Allsun finds her voice.

"You!" Pierre tries to laugh, but can manage only a rasping wheeze.

Outside on the Tundra Buggy deck, Suzuki gives the crew the thumbs up and Gord tells him and Allsun, "He just stopped ... the bear, like someone threw a switch. He just lay down and rubbed his head, sliding those snowshoe paws delicately over his eyes. He was good enough to lie there and let us tape him for quite a time before he moved on."

"How long would you say it took the bear to regain its faculties?" Suzuki asks Gord.

"I'd estimate five to seven minutes." Gord glances at the camera, measuring time in video tape.

"Three quarters of a can of pepper spray and he recovers in seven minutes. Not bad, especially considering he got half of that at close range. A helluva lot closer than I'd ever want to be to a charging polar bear."

LEAVING THE CAPE, Conrad flies south, the Jet Ranger's shadow slipping over tundra then over taiga. The maternity dens are in a taiga area—patches of black spruce on banks of earth into which the female polar bears can dig and snow can drift—inland from Hudson Bay about thirty-five miles.

Conrad buzzes a couple of subadult bears grazing on kelp, both with coats stained yellow from rolling around in their banquet. Allsun slides the panel in the middle of the window back and photographs as the helicopter comes up on them. The two bears sit down.

"I bet they've been darted before," Conrad says into the microphone attached to his earphones.

"Why do you think so?" Allsun sends back, conscious of the headset that attenuates the terrific noise of the rotor blades whirling like demon dancers to the powerful tune of a turbine engine weighing no more than a 125 pounds.

"They know what part of their anatomy is a target. They're protecting their butts, instead of running away." Conrad laughs—an explosive sound in the headset. He knows better than to subject his passengers to earphone laughter, but he can't help himself. He's just so damn happy to have Allsun on board. And she specifically asked to come. That has to be a good sign.

"Did you ever have one stand on its hind legs and bat at the chopper?" she asks.

"Yeah, fearless buggers." Conrad's head is turned, his attention focused on the bears below.

"You have to wonder what goes on in their minds ..."

"Jud," Conrad breaks in, "do you want to go down for these two?"

"No. Got the binoculars on them, they're tagged."

"Sorry, Allsun, you were saying?" Conrad gradually pulls up the collective to adjust the pitch on the blades, then eases the cyclic forward to take them out. The helicopter lifts away from the bears. They stand.

"Conrad," Jud is hailing him, "they're numbered. Can we get a look?"

Conrad circles as if leaving. This encourages the bears to run. Then quickly he comes back in on them so Jud can record the numbers painted on their flanks.

"Sorry?" Conrad says again.

"Nothing really, I was just thinking out loud." Allsun is distracted as well, trying to get shots of the dyed bears. How strange they look: defiled, defined by numbers until their hair falls out in the spring and they go back to being themselves, no longer data points.

"Yeah?" Conrad's inducement to continue the conversation. He wants to hear what she thinks.

"Is the helicopter some giant insect or bird, you know, to them?" She picks up the thread of her thoughts. "Something from the polar bears' Pleistocene past?"

"Their what? Plasticine?" Conrad swings the helicopter back on course.

"Yeah, the age of model-making." Allsun laughs. "The Pleistocene epoch, Conrad." She repeats, her tone suggesting she wasn't laughing at him. "A million years ago when there were giant mammals . . . you know, woolly mammoths, cave bears, giant beaver."

"Giant polar bears?" Conrad sounds surprised.

"No, polar bears aren't that old," Jud corrects. "We don't know for sure when polar bears started to evolve from brown bears. Oldest fossil is one hundred thousand years." He hoists the binoculars to survey ahead of the retreating landscape.

Richard Rowan studies Jud's reflection in the window. It looks as if Jud has raised the field glasses to look for archeological proof. Richard has done some digging of his own, but he hasn't got to the bones, the proof of what he believes he knows about Jud.

"That fossil . . . dug up in London, England, of all places," Allsun adds, not about to be corrected by Jud. "Explain that!" Polar bear evolution is a mystery as far as she's concerned.

"So, polar bears are really white grizzly bears?" Conrad sounds disappointed. "Is that what you're saying?"

"No," Jud is emphatic. "Ursus arctos—"

"Bear, bear, in Latin and Greek." Allsun is gunning for Jud. "Bear of bears in two languages, Conrad."

"Ursus arctos," Jud continues peevishly, "brown or grizzly bears and Ursus maritimus, polar bears . . . same genus, which means they can mate successfully and have . . . in zoos. Another perverse experiment that couldn't wait for genetic testing."

"What do you mean, perverse?" Richard hopes Jud will place his credo on the table, hopes Jud will slip up. That's why he came along on this survey, to apply some pressure, if only by his presence.

"Just what I said. It satisfied human curiosity, that's all, while creating animals condemned to live their whole lives in zoos. If zoos were abolished tomorrow, there is no way these hybrid offspring could be released into the wild," Jud says from behind the binoculars. He looks as impersonal as a large-eyed insect.

"Why?" Conrad sounds disconcerted, which must be gratifying to Jud.

"They'd contaminate the gene pool." Jud's tone is now matter-of-fact.

Allsun, angered by Jud's sanctimonious attitude, gets him in her sights. "So, according to you, polar bears and brown bears don't mate in the wild?"

"There's no documentation to prove they do." This is a seemingly neutral scientific statement, but it reveals Jud's narrow view of science.

"That's not what the people of the North say. And

they've been studying bears longer than anyone." Allsun challenges him to throw his brand of science in the face of experience.

"Female with cubs at twelve o'clock," Conrad alerts them.

Jud gets a bead on the white bears with the binoculars.

"Well?" Conrad finally asks.

From behind his field glasses, Jud makes the call. "No tags. We'll go down," he says.

Conrad takes the chopper into where Jud can get a good look at the bears and estimate how much each one weighs.

Allsun turns to watch as Jud selects a Cap-Chur dart and loads it into a dart rifle with a name as long as the barrel: Extra Long Range (Powder) Projector. The arsenal of darts sits ready in a metal case arranged according to size and dosage.

Jud slides open his window, takes the dart rifle and sights in the mother bear as Conrad comes in over top of the fleeing family. Jud will aim for the rump or shoulder in order to place the needle in muscle. Rich in blood vessels, muscle transfers the drug into the bloodstream quickly.

He hits her in the upper part of the left leg near the tail.

"Good shot," Conrad remarks.

Jud reloads.

"Jud, we're taking the cubs from the air?" Conrad confirms.

"Yeah, they're too big to chance it on the ground."

"That's what I thought." Conrad backs off as the mother bear begins to slow, the cubs staying with her.

"Smaller targets," Richard comments. He wonders what kind of field training Jud has had. This is nothing like what he got from LIB in the impenetrable forests of Oregon. It takes considerable practice to assemble and fill darts, and to get a feel for the range and trajectory of the dart rifle. It's not child's play. A dart gun is a lethal weapon.

As if in concert with his own thoughts, Richard hears Conrad explain to Allsun, "It's pretty much a syringe with a gun powder cartridge behind it. There are different .22 blank loads, color-coded according to strength. For darting from a chopper, it's best to use a low-medium charge, color-coded brown or green. Anything with a higher charge could injure the bear, piercing the skin with more than the needle. But marksmanship is crucial . . . shooting the bear in the rib cage, abdomen, or spine could cause real harm."

Allsun is making notes. "Can you fill me in on the needle and the drug?" she asks Conrad.

Conrad is happy to show off what he's learned from years of taking bear biologists out on the land. "Gotta choose the right needle length, the right amount of the immobilization drug, for the size of bear you're darting. For example, the darts used on polar bears are 5-, 7-, and 10-ml with needles of 1.5–5 cm. So an adult female like we just got would probably take 7 cc's of reconstituted Telazol."

"Reconstituted? What do you mean by that? And what's Telazol?" Allsun asks as she gets ready to photograph the darting of the cubs.

Conrad is bringing the chopper into range. "Telazol's a powder that has to be mixed with sterile water. It's an aesthetic, anticonvulsant and muscle relaxant."

Jud doesn't miss.

This is no surprise to Richard. He's been warned about Jud Ash's skill with guns.

Once all three bears are darted, Conrad lifts and banks away. "If Jud had missed, that would have been it. We would've backed off. Can't chase polar bears for more than five minutes. They overheat really fast with those dense coats and layers of fat. Send them into hyperthermia ... heat distress."

The group retreats to watch from the air as the Telazol goes to work. The bears have stopped running. Instead, they are high-stepping, like careful inebriates, albeit ones on all fours in white fur coats.

First one cub, then the other, sits down, its hind legs having collapsed. They lick their lips, then lie down as the front legs become powerless.

Their mother turns back drunkenly, trying in desperation to stay upright to protect her cubs. She collapses as well, licking her lips until she loses movement in her head, neck and finally her tongue. The tongue is an indicator that she's under.

Conrad moves in and sets down.

It had been decided earlier that Allsun would act as armed guard while Jud and Conrad collected data and marked the bears. Richard Rowan could photograph.

The group approaches the mother bear from the rear. Jud is carrying the immobilization kit. Conrad has a ski pole. They're all shouting, a strange chorus of improvised lyrics. Conrad prods the mother bear several times with the ski pole. There is no response to this strange greeting.

Similarly, the cubs are prodded to make sure they are asleep. Conrad checks to see that the bears are lying comfortably and breathing properly. He then retrieves the dart from the flank of the mother bear, removes the dart's tail piece and pushes the rubber plunger down the barrel to see if the drug was completely injected.

Jud opens the immobilization kit and takes out three tea towels.

Slinging the rifle over her shoulder, Allsun lifts her camera. "What is this, the teddy bears' picnic?" she asks Jud.

Nothing remotely like a smile crosses his face. "To cover their eyes," is all he says.

"Why?" she persists, as she takes shots of him and the bears.

"They'll be less stressed if they can't see us," he says from where he is bent over the immobilization kit, removing the equipment he needs.

"A new one on me." Conrad would like to know more.

Jud doesn't bother to enlighten him.

Richard rapidly circles and shoots.

"No rush," Conrad says to Richard as he checks the time. "We have a window of about fifty minutes to safely handle the bears. There was no drug left in the darts."

Jud passes Conrad one end of a measuring tape that they slide under the female bear to a position behind her front legs. They measure her girth to get a number that can be checked against a table in order to establish her weight.

While Conrad removes the tattooing gear from the immobilization kit, Jud finds a syringe. Jud has left Conrad the messy job of applying green tattoo ink to the female's upper lip on the inside above the large canine tooth. Jud takes a blood sample from her shoulder. Conrad, his fingers now dyed government green, stamps her gum with tattoo pliers, leaving a permanent number that identifies her and only her across the polar countries.

Richard takes close-ups of the tattooing. He's enthralled by the contrasting pink gums and black lips and tongue of the bear, not to mention overlapping canine teeth the length of Conrad's thumb.

Jud clips white tags to the bears' ears. In the international world of polar bears, she is X199991. So say her tags and the green cipher on the inside of her lip.

Jud has brought calipers to measure the bears' skulls for some independent research he has undertaken. He hands Richard the squeeze bottle of Lady Clairol Burgundy Babe, so Richard can also get his hands dirty painting a number on her rump. The number must be large enough to be seen from the air. This way, she won't be recaptured, but her movements can be recorded.

Jud and Conrad repeat the data-collecting procedure on the cubs. They are the size, if not the color, of Newfoundland Retrievers. Richard is down on his knees, then flat on his stomach shooting everything they do. Allsun photographs the photographer, when she's not scouting for intruders.

As they work quickly on the second cub, Richard puts his camera aside so he can caress this young marvel with his hand instead of his eye. The fur is fine and he's immediately reminded of how the camera removes him from the reality of his other senses. He closes his eyes, allowing his fingers to explore. He listens to the cub's breathing, takes his own deep breath full of cold, the chemical smell of dye and the strong odor of animal fear. There is a contradiction in the softness beneath his fingers and the sharp scent of fight-or-flight hormones. This conjures the image of Inuit hunters who prize polar bear fur above all else, primarily for its utility in pants, bed robes and sled runners, but also as a symbol of their self-sufficiency. He remembers reading that a wife advertised her husband's hunting prowess by trimming her boots with the long hair from a polar bear's foreleg.

Allsun notices the look of disdain on Jud's face as he watches Richard attempt to connect with the cub.

Jud glances at his watch as he starts to repack the immobilization kit. With everything in order, he retrieves the squeeze bottle of hair dye. Bending to the cubs' pristine fur, whiter than their mothers', Jud inscribes numbers on these blank pages with color bolder than blood.

Putting the bottle back, Jud takes out the pliers and hands them to Richard in a manner reminiscent of the cold efficiency of the operating theatre. "Need a tooth from the female."

Richard looks from the pliers to Jud. He's not sure what Jud's playing at. "I'm no dentist," he says with a smile.

"You'll do. It's just a small tooth directly behind the long canine." Jud is gauging Richard's reluctance. "Once in a lifetime opportunity," he adds.

"Sure, let's give it a shot." Richard has to admit to himself the idea of getting down and dirty with Nanuk of the North excites him. But at Jud Ash's invitation? "You'll have to coach me," he says to Jud, who has already turned away.

"Conrad will show you what to do." Jud walks the immobilization kit over to the helicopter.

Conrad directs Richard to take hold of the bear's snout and lift the upper jaw from behind the nose. "Okay, roll back the lip and have a look. Pretty impressive, eh? See, behind the big canine there's a space, then a tiny little tooth in front of the incisors. You're going for the little tooth. It comes out pretty easy."

As Richard switches his grip on the bear to his left hand so he can wield the pliers in his right, Conrad explains that the tooth is not used for chewing. The space behind the canines is called the diastema. The incisors are as sharp as broken glass and can strip the skin off a walrus or a seal.

Richard has the tooth. He stares, fascinated by the small bit of rare ivory in the steel grip of the needle-nose pliers. He releases the bear's upper jaw. As he drops the extracted tooth into his open palm, he screams.

The bear has sunk a long canine through the palm of his left hand. She holds the martyred hand in her jaws, too drugged to exert the bone-crushing strength of that powerful living trap. Her eyes roll in their sockets. She's coming out of the anaesthetic.

Grasping the upper jaw, Conrad pulls. The bear instinctively tightens her grip. Richard cries out. He stares in horror as the bear focuses on him.

Conrad reaches for the pliers and strikes the bear on her sensitive nose with the long-handled steel tool. Surprised, the bear releases her grip just long enough for Richard to pull free. Blood spurts onto the snow. Richard rocks back on his heels, cradling his hand.

The bear's tongue flicks out, licking the blood off her lip, a sign she's gaining control of her motor movements.

Allsun lifts the Winchester to her shoulder, taking aim

at the bear. "Conrad, get him out of there!" she shouts.

They make a dash for the helicopter as five hundred pounds of antagonized mother bear pushes up on her front legs.

They're strapping in as Conrad flips switches and checks his watch. Odd; unless he miscalculated, she should have been under for at least another ten minutes. There is that moment of maddening delay while the blades wind up. The interminable whine of the turbine before its power transforms solid rotors to a blur. Then the blades beat above the sound of their hearts. The polar bear stands. They lift off.

Allsun is in the back seat with Richard. She has the first-aid kit open in her lap and she's treating what is a clean-cut puncture wound. "You're going to need a tetanus shot," she tells him.

"Had one two weeks ago. Stepped on a nail."

Allsun takes a long look at him. He doesn't seem to be in shock. "Now you got two out of four," she teases. "Hell of a mortification."

"How'd you know I'm Catholic?" Richard is trying to join in, make light.

"The bear. She was so obliging. Helping you toward beatification."

"God works in mysterious ways." Richard holds his left hand high as if to give a pontifical wave.

Conrad's voice comes over the headset. "You want to turn back?"

"Richard's call," Jud says.

His bandaged hand elevated, Richard decides not to give Jud the satisfaction. "We've come this far. I can manage."

By the time they've reached the edge of a small inland lake, Jud has spotted four other bears, all tagged, two with dye jobs. A slope rises from the scrub on the shore of the lake. The top of the slope sports a five o'clock shadow of black spruce. Dug into this bank below the trees are maternity dens, the entrances obvious because there has been no new snow to fill and hide them.

Conrad flies low along the slope. The vibration from the chopper triggers tiny avalanches that scar the white, canting face. It takes another pass by the helicopter to raise three pregnant sows from what is not a deep sleep. "Bears are not true hibernators in the way bats or rodents are," he tells them. "After all, the females need to be conscious enough to give birth, nurse their young, defend themselves."

Allsun has the sense that Conrad is speaking directly to her. She feels obliged to keep the conversation going. "Their heart beat slows from eighty to twenty-seven beats per minute, but their body temperature stays normal ... 98.6 degrees Fahrenheit. I remember this stuff on body temperature because it fits with the Inuit belief that polar bears are really humans in disguise." Allsun listens to herself. This conversation has the ring of a first date. Holy crow!

"And how do you take a polar bear's temperature?" Richard asks.

"Very carefully," Conrad laughs at this old joke.

"I can just imagine Guy out on the tundra trying to introduce a six hundred-pound bear to a rectal thermometer." Allsun joins Conrad in the banter.

"They did some of that testing at Churchill." Conrad is nothing if not well informed. "Built a physiology lab in one of the abandoned buildings on the old base . . . a Norwegian scientist by the name of Nils Øritsland. Put polar bears on treadmills in a respiration chamber and measured temperature, heart rate, breathing, oxygen and carbon dioxide. Never did find out how he got the lords of the North to cooperate."

Below the helicopter, the three pregnant bears are running up the slope toward the black spruce. Conrad maneuvers to cut off their retreat into the trees.

Quickly Jud opens the metal case containing the tranquilizer darts and loads the rifle.

This time Jud is in the front seat. Conrad now has a chance to examine the darts Jud is using. Conrad notices that Jud has selected a 9-cc dart, which is suitable for an adult male. The pregnant bears are fat, probably weighing an average of 825 pounds. Conrad reviews Jud's choice.

He takes another hard look at the tranqu-kit. It contains Cap-Chur darts that are reusable and consequently require assemblage, unlike the disposable Pneu-Dart System. He knows that to fill a Pneu-Dart you insert the needle of a syringe into the dart needle, whereas the Cap-Chur dart needs a light coating of silicone lubricant on the rubber plunger before the barrel is filled with the drug, as well as silicone on the o-rings of the feathered tailpiece and needle to create a proper seal. When the drug solution does not completely fill the barrel of the Cap-Chur dart, it must be topped up with sterile water. All of this has to be done ahead of time, before they get into the air. Conrad would like to know who prepared these darts. Was it Guy or Jud? In Conrad's mind, there's no way the sow that grabbed Richard should have come around in thirty-eight minutes. Either Jud miscalculated her weight or the darts don't contain enough drug.

When they land, Conrad makes a point of checking his watch. He's wondering how much tranquilizer drug and how much sterile water was in the darts used on the pregnant females. Are they going to come around early too?

Collecting data and marking the bears is done in short order, without incident. Richard tries for shots, but is forced to put his camera down when blood soaks through his bandage.

On the way back to camp, Conrad swings out over the Bay beyond the tower to check the ice. It's not Henry Hudson's bay that alerts him to freeze-up conditions, it's the twenty-three bears he flies over. Like so many sunbathers at the shore, the polar bears lounge on the gravel shingle or pad about and roll on the newly formed ice as if playing in gentle waves. On the horizon are what could be Inukshuk, the "standing man" stone cairns that mark invisible paths across the tundra. Conrad knows better. What he's seeing in the distance are polar bears migrating out to the edge of the ice, pulled by the promise of a storm in the air, as if they were compass needles in the presence of magnetic north.

THERE'S A KIND of electricity in Churchill's Legion Hall tonight, a frenetic hum that builds just before bad weather. Conrad has noticed this hum before. He sips his shandy from a beer glass and ponders just what to tell Karen Klassen of his suspicions. She's off duty. They're chewing the fat. He can measure out his thoughts by the glass.

"That guy from CBC was in and out of here like a dose of salts." Karen keeps track of who's in her town and who isn't. Conrad is her major pipeline.

"Suzuki. Left early. Supposed to go south tomorrow. Didn't want to get caught up here with the weather coming in. Nice fellow. Real smart guy, you know." Conrad doesn't want her to think David Suzuki has anything against Churchill.

"So what about those scientists left out at the Cape? They coming in too?" In moving on, she has accepted Conrad's endorsement of those Toronto TV people.

"Yeah, tomorrow morning. This coming storm will be the end of the bears. They'll be gonzo. Most of them are already out on the Bay." Conrad is watching the bubbles in his glass rise to the surface like seals under the ice. "Someone should warn the seals."

"So, what's on your mind?" Karen is looking straight at him.

"There was another accident today," Conrad begins. Karen waits. "That American photographer got his hand chewed when we were working on a drugged bear."

"Bad?"

"No, not really, it wasn't mangled or anything. Just a canine puncture."

"And?"

"The bear came around too soon."

"What went wrong?"

"I don't know, not for sure. But I sent one of the tranquilizer darts south on the flight that took Suzuki out. Gave it to the pilot; he's going to deliver it to a government biologist I know in Winnipeg." Conrad lays out his suspicions on the table between them, then raises his glass.

"So you stole a dart with a drug in it and put it on an airplane, have I got that right?" She takes a swig of beer and holds it in her mouth before swallowing. Early in their friendship Conrad had noticed this little habit and asked her about it. "Slow and easy," she had said. "Keeps me from drinking too much."

"Yeah, I want to know how much Telazol was used. I want to know if the dart was filled properly." His words are as clear and crisp as the ginger ale he adds to his beer.

"And if it wasn't? Human error?" Karen has heard the edge in his voice. There is more than curiosity or friendly concern driving Conrad. Somehow this is personal.

"Maybe, but there hasn't been a bear research accident, let alone a death, in years. Then all of a sudden at the Cape we got . . . geez, we got all hell breaking loose." Conrad thinks of Allsun still out there. "I just got this feeling. I don't like it."

"What about Mr. Ford? Does your feeling include what happened to him?"

"I don't know. I wasn't out there the night he was killed. But he knew the score. Guy made sure that Chuck understood the ground was off limits. I mean this Ford, he was an experienced guy. He'd been making nature shows for at least two decades. Doesn't make sense that he'd go outside, let alone down the tower, in the middle of the night."

"Unless he's pissed."

"Was he?"

"Don't have the report yet."

Conrad thinks about asking her to put a rush on it, maybe put a call into the medical examiner. Then he realizes she'll do it anyway, now that they've talked.

"So, Conrad, you know these people. Who would want to cause trouble?" Karen is starting to dig deeper.

"I know Guy and Neal. Jud and Allsun I just met this week. Guy and Neal have a history, I know that. Allsun is a friend of theirs. This Jud's a student hired to help with the research. I found out Jud filled the Cap-Chur darts we were using today."

"So? If he's a student, maybe he got the dosage wrong?" She's playing devil's advocate. What does Conrad really have?

"Yeah, could be. But there's something about him—"

"You're not getting bushed, are you? The Force warns us about paranoia running rampant in the Great White North."

"You got a lot of gall. I was living up here before you were a gleam in your daddy's eye." Now he's worried she's not taking him seriously.

"Don't pull the silver fox routine with me. Old Karl deLeeuw makes you look like a youngster and he went off his nut out on his trapline."

"Do something for me?" Conrad gives Karen a look she can't doubt. "Soon, real soon, see what you can get from the medical examiner on Chuck Ford. Okay?"

"Sure. You really do think something's going on, don't you?"

"Yeah, but don't ask me what."

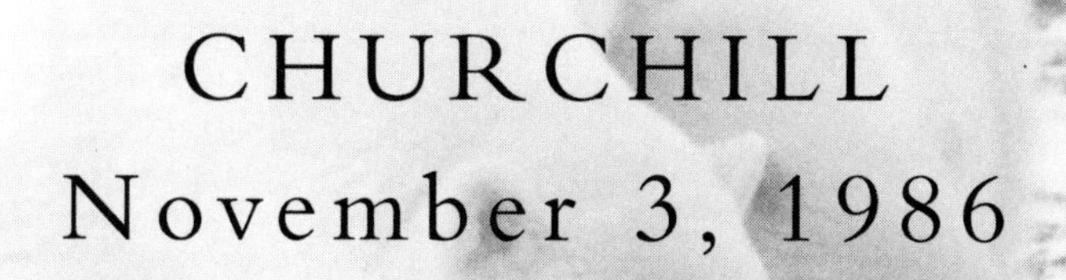

CHURCHILL
November 3, 1986

THE CHURCHILL CAFÉ is like a ship frozen into the Arctic ice. Beyond windows thick with frost, the world outside is white and featureless. Every action, every word inside the small box of a building is amplified to compete with the blasting wind.

The Cape crew is not fazed by the cramped café, but they find the heat stifling. They're used to rooms the temperature of iceboxes. Doesn't matter. They shed layers of clothing—nothing short of a kitchen fire is going to shift them out of there. Once they had got a whiff of brewed coffee, frying bacon, burnt toast, the world became a kinder place.

"The storm's a hummer, alright," Guy says into the large mug of coffee he's inhaling.

"Only at the Cape," Conrad counters. "In Churchill it's a bummer." He gets his easy laugh. Everyone seems in high spirits, in spite of all that has happened. "Before I forget," Conrad searches his pockets for a note, "Dr. Thomas left a message with my answering service . . . 'Allsun, Neal, your test results won't be back for a week. Will forward to your Calgary physicians.'"

Their clubhouse sandwiches arrive, each one stacked so high it's teetering on the plate. French fries are piled like kindling around towers of sourdough bread, back bacon, chicken breast, cheese and assorted vegetable matter. Guy's not sure he'd recognize lettuce if he saw it.

"So, did you get what you needed?" Conrad asks Guy.

"It's all here."

"No, I mean the Cape, your research." Conrad shakes his head at how quickly deprivation refocuses human interest in the basics.

Guy glances at Neal. "It'll have to do."

"Tough time this year." Conrad wants the others to recognize that the last few days are the exception, not the rule. This hasn't been a typical Cape research camp experience.

"Yeah, and it ain't going to get any easier." Guy puts his head down and concentrates on his food.

Conrad excuses himself and makes for the back of the café. Passing the washrooms, he continues down the passage to a door marked PRIVATE. He opens it without knocking and disappears inside.

When he returns to the table, the bill is being paid. "So where can I drop you?" he asks, trying not to sound impatient.

Guy looks up from the money he is counting. "Neal and I are just going next door to the Arctic Inn. We've got some calls to make."

"Jud?" Conrad is offering, but he has got someplace to be.

"I can walk," Jud says.

"Suit yourself."

"Allsun, you want to take a drive?" Conrad has purposely asked her last. "I've got an errand to run."

Neal is alert to Conrad's casual invitation. He looks openly from Conrad to Allsun.

"Sure," she says to Conrad. As they leave, she turns to Neal and Guy. "Buy you a beer at the Legion in a couple of hours?"

"Yeah, we should know how deep a sling our asses are in by then," Guy says. "Make it two beer."

Neal says nothing, not even goodbye.

THE WIND OUTSIDE the door of the Churchill Café slams them so hard that Allsun stumbles into Conrad. He wraps an arm around her shoulder and they make a dash for his Bronco. He opens the driver's side door, bracing it from the outside with his whole body as if it were a long Roman shield held against the blows of an enemy. Allsun jumps in, scuttles across the bucket seat and over the stick shift. Now on the inside of the door, it is all Conrad can do to pull it shut.

"That was invigorating," Conrad remarks as he starts the truck.

"Walk in the park."

They laugh, a little at a loss to find themselves together, alone.

"So, where are we going?" Allsun asks. "Or is this a mystery tour?" She's trying to keep it light.

Instead of pulling onto the deserted street, Conrad turns to her. "I just called Cst. Klassen." Allsun nods. "I'm on my way to see her."

"You in trouble?" Allsun is worried by the change in Conrad's expression.

"Me? No." He notes the look of concern on her face

and is gratified, although he didn't mean to mislead her. "But the trouble at the Cape ... well, let's just say I figure there might have been more than bad luck at work."

"What's going on?"

"All I know for sure is that when we did the survey down to Owl River at least one, probably two, of the tranquilizer darts didn't have enough Telazol in the solution." Conrad scrutinizes her face to see if she understands the implications. "The bear that chomped Richard's hand was underdrugged."

"How do you know this?" Allsun is struggling to grasp his meaning.

"I had a dart from the kit analyzed."

"You what?"

"I've worked with drugged bears for nearly ten years. I know how these immobilization drugs take. The ratio of Telazol to the number of minutes a bear's out . . . it's pretty much a given." Allsun is about to speak and Conrad holds up a hand. "Guy didn't make up the darts for the survey. Jud did."

"Yeah, but—"

"Jud moves the observation cage . . . the latch breaks. Jud's hackles go up when Richard Rowan's around. After I talk to Karen, we're going to go find Richard." Conrad aims the truck into the vortex of snow that marks the street.

THE LEGION SHOULD be quiet this time of day. That's what Jud had expected, but now he finds that the storm has driven people to seek refuge in a smoke and a glass. He decides against the public telephones beside the johns—too much traffic. Near the main entrance is a sign pointing to a set of stairs leading down to a banquet hall. Just maybe? He finds a pay phone. And privacy. He dials the operator. A collect call to Trevor Ash.

"Guess you heard about Chuck Ford's unfortunate accident?" Jud listens hard. And there it is—the censure mixed in with the sanctimonious shit his father is famous for and Jud hates more than life. "I know what you said. Now shut up and listen to me. I killed Chuck Ford. Not for you, you arrogant bastard. I killed him for me. Me and LIB. You sacrificed me once to your ambitions. Will you do it again? I've always wanted to know." Jud slams the head of the receiver down onto the hook.

At the top of the stairs Jud hears voices he recognizes. He stops out of sight to listen. "The merde's hit the fan, that's for damn sure. Calling it an international fucking incident. Not to mention what the media's doing with the bear kill. There's going to be bureaucrats coming at us faster than—"

"Take it easy, Guy. We've been in tight spots before. We'll get through this."

"We, Neal? You don't have to take the heat for this. It's my project, you can step away."

"Too much at stake."

"To stay?"

"No, to go. Years of good research buried under politics ... no way, Guy. This is important work. No, this is vital work. Just keep remembering that."

CST. KAREN KLASSEN leads Conrad through the RCMP detachment to her boss's office—he's gone to the mayor's lunch in honor of Bishop Robidoux. Karen picks up coffees for them on the way. Allsun sits in the waiting room with a Styrofoam cup of her own.

"You first," Karen says as she wheels the chair from behind the desk.

"I was right about the dart on both counts." He sits opposite her.

"Well, I know it's meaningful to you, Conrad. But Jud could claim it was an accident due to inexperience. Who's to say different?" Karen blows on her coffee to cool the dark pool so she can sip and hold it in her mouth.

Conrad grimaces. The coffee's bad enough when it's scalding. "Have you heard from the medical examiner?"

"We had a talk. Remember, this is stuff you shouldn't rightfully know about." She pauses to sip, hold, and let her warning sink in. "He's telling me Chuck took a blow to the back of the head. But he figures it's not from being dragged across the tundra by a bear. Maybe the bear beat him up. You know how polars have a way of grabbing and shaking seals to death."

"Christ!" Conrad stares at her.

"Something else," she says, waiting for him to wrap his head around the idea of murder at the Cape. "I had a visit from that American who has been out at the camp. He tells me this Jud Ash attacked a man during a break and enter at the university in Calgary. The man's still in a coma." Karen registers the look of shock on Conrad's face. "That's right. Your friend Allsun's husband. How's that for karma?"

"How does he know this?"

"He's a journalist. He gets anonymous tips. That's his story."

"I didn't think he was that kind of journalist. Investigative or whatever it's called. He takes pictures, for god's sake." Conrad is finding it hard to come to terms with more deception.

"I called Calgary on it. They want me to ask Jud Ash a few questions. But I'd like to talk to Allsun first." Karen sees alarm flash across Conrad's eyes. "Background. She can fill me in."

JUD MAPS HIS plan on the grid of acoustic tiles that make up the ceiling of his hotel room. Not for the first time has he plotted this course, but now it's confirmed. He should have killed his father when he had the chance. But his chance will come again and there will be no mistaking Trevor Ash for what he is. These past years with his father ... Jud thinks of himself as a cobra in a basket. His father is a master charmer, skilled in bending wills, calling the tune. But this time his father has sold an empty basket.

That hick of a Mountie can't keep him here. Whatever Trevor has told her about the LIB raid in Calgary, there's no way she or anyone else can place him there. He has been well trained in covering his tracks, thanks to the departed Mr. Ford and his school of guerrilla warfare. The storm quits, he's on the first plane out of Churchill, out of Canada—no home or native land to him.

IN THE ROOM above the ceiling Jud is staring at, Richard Rowan glances at the clock radio. It's time. He turns the volume on the radio up a notch. The phone rings.

"Rowan here."

He listens.

"What do you expect me to do with this information?" Richard Rowan says into the phone. His source knows more about him than he realized. Just what kind of network does this guy have?

He hangs up the phone. Absently he reaches for the radio dial. The weather report predicts the blizzard will blow itself out by tomorrow morning.

A knock at the door has Richard shoving his notebook between the mattress and box spring of his bed. Through the peephole in the door he recognizes the helicopter pilot. He opens the door to Conrad and finds Allsun there as well.

"Hi. What's up? We going for a drink?" Richard keeps them at the threshold of his room.

"Can we come in." Conrad does not pose this as a question.

"Sure, sure. Let me clear off the chairs." Richard moves into the room, making busy while he tries to get a handle on the situation.

"No need. This won't take long." Conrad remains standing.

"So what's on your mind?"

"The Mounties can't hold him."

"Pardon?"

"How did you know about my husband?" Allsun is wound so tight, there's bound to be an explosion.

Richard studies the minefield. "I know about Jud. And what I know is very little. Until I came here, I'd never heard of him."

Conrad's eyes have gone stony. "I want a straight

answer for a straight question. Who told you Jud attacked Damon?"

Damon's name, word made flesh before her eyes. Allsun takes a single step and, with remarkable force, body slams Richard Rowan into the wall.

A stunned silence prevails until Allsun steps away, but not before she has pinned Richard there with her eyes. He has looked on a lot of pain in his time. He knows the real thing when he sees it.

"I came up here because of Chuck Ford. I've been piecing together a story on him for a couple of years. When I get out to the camp, I notice there's something between him and this Jud Ash. After my adventure in the observation cage," Richard raises an eyebrow, indicating that, as far as he's concerned, it was no accident, "we came back into Churchill and I made a few calls from your office at the hangar. I got someone to check up on Jud. When you dropped me off here at the Inn, there was a message waiting for me. It had been here for twenty-four hours. I called the number. I was told about the attack at the university and Jud's part in it. That was all I got out of the caller." What Richard fails to mention is that his anonymous caller has also been feeding him information on Chuck Ford for several months. "I haven't been able to verify the story."

"So, it could be a hoax? What kind of bullshit is that?" Conrad steps in close, keeping Richard against the wall.

"I'm telling you what I know. Just like I told the officer. I figured she might want to pass it along to whoever is investigating your husband's case." Richard looks beyond Conrad in an appeal to Allsun. He'd like to be able to tell her that he believes Jud did her husband. That just before they arrived at his door, he put it all together with the help of his informant: out there in the barren lands Jud Ash mounted a coup. According to the man on the telephone, Jud killed Chuck Ford and set in motion a takeover of LIB by his unit.

Richard Rowan had set out to unmask the host of *Wild World* as the head of a underground army bent on reducing dams to rumble, oil fields to cinders, mines to forgotten scars on the face of the earth. Now he was covering a war.

ALLSUN AND CONRAD slide another round Legion Hall table in beside Guy and Neal. They drag two heavy western saloon chairs across a hallucinogenic carpet of orange and brown blossoms outlined in black. As spongy as a mushroom and smelling of yeast, it's a wall-to-wall artifact of the seventies. Its flowered pattern seems to entrance the group. Subdued, they stare at the floor.

This is how Richard Rowan finds them. "So, whose dog died?" he asks.

They make room for him. Guy is the first to speak. "The gang's all here except Jud. Where is that boy?"

Conrad inspects Richard. "You seen Jud?" he asks the man he believes is holding out on them.

"Back at the Inn would be my guess." Richard understands that Conrad and Allsun are suspicious. But the whole story, as he knows it, is of no use to them. Until it is corroborated, the law can't touch Jud.

Richard fills the dead air. "Looks like the weather's going to break tonight. What do you think, Conrad, will there be a plane out of here tomorrow morning?"

"A good chance," Conrad says. "You had enough of the North?"

"Never a dull moment." Richard holds up his bandaged hand. "Even got a souvenir." Tension charges the air like invisible sparks of static electricity.

RICHARD ROWAN THINKS of himself as a war correspondent as he boards a plane at Churchill's airport and takes a seat beside Jud Ash.

CAPE CHURCHILL

October 30, 1987

THE TUNDRA BUGGY AT THE research camp this year has a fresh coat of yellow paint on the inside walls. Much better than the white walls of last year. The Buggy bunkhouse somehow seems warmer, an illusion or perhaps a delusion, Allsun thinks, as she watches condensation freeze on the ceiling. To conserve on propane, they've turned the furnace down to the lowest setting and taken to their bunks. Cocooned in their sleeping bags, they look like so many alien pupae stored separately on the shelves of an incubator. They certainly could be some monstrous experiment gone wrong and jettisoned into the wilderness. Allsun chuckles to herself at the thought.

"What's so funny?" Guy asks, as his head bobs up out of the shiny blue waves of his sleeping bag like a seal at a breathing hole.

"Just thinking." Allsun is not about to introduce this group to the science fiction she has been reading lately.

"Come on, Al. Don't hold out on us. You're among friends." Neal takes yet another opportunity to remind Conrad of his long-standing friendship with Allsun.

Earlier in the day, when Allsun and Conrad arrived at the Cape, Neal hadn't wasted any time in letting Conrad know that he had hired Allsun to document the development of something Neal calls CapSeek. In the new year, the testing would take them to Auburn University in Alabama and then to a bayou outside New Orleans.

Allsun finally answers Neal. "You guys should be studying human behavior. It's humans who keep getting it wrong, not the bears." She's not sure this is what she meant to say. But out here on the tundra with the polar bears, her life, her friends' lives seem so messy, so complicated.

"Christ, no. I study the bears so I can get away from people." A nylon hiss comes from Guy's bunk as he shifts, trying to get comfortable—a losing battle.

"In spades after this past year." Neal's voice is muffled as he leans over the edge of his bunk to fish out a small travel bag. "Here it is! Let's drink to that."

"To what?" Guy demands. "Not that I'm passing up the offer."

"To vindication!" Neal unscrews the top on a partial bottle of Glenfiddich. Loath to abandon his newly warmed nest to get cups, he takes a swig from the tall, three-sided bottle and passes it to Allsun in the next bunk.

"I'll drink to that, but what does it mean?" She tips the bottle of single malt and rays from the bulb over the door dance inside the green glass like northern lights.

"What it means is that the inquisition is over. Guy held out, never signed a phony confession, despite bureaucratic torture. They owe him an apology, which he'll never get. But at least he got an explanation of sorts." Neal pauses as the bottle comes back down the line to him. "The Bear Safety Program, it's back on track, there's funding, a new minister, industry's on board. Life is good."

Conrad listens between the lines of Neal's little speech and he hears Neal's support for Guy. In one of her letters, Allsun had written that Guy and Neal were working together and the friendship was on the mend. He's happy for Guy. He knows how Jane's death had preyed on his mind. Conrad had pointed out in one of his many talks with Guy that, even if he hadn't looked away for a split second, he couldn't have got a shot off in time to save her. Jane's accident could be blamed on bad camp design, the very thing Guy and Neal are now working on.

"Have you heard anything more?" Allsun asks, well aware that she probably knows at least as much as or more than the police detectives handling Damon's case do.

"Last I heard," Guy figures he's out of the government's information loop now, "the FBI are looking for Jud."

Conrad speaks up, telling the others what he has already told Allsun. "Heard from Karen Klassen. She got transferred to Winnipeg. The RCMP have been helping the FBI put a case together against Jud for Chuck's death and the attack on Damon. What has really got them worried is this eco-terrorist outfit he's a part of... looks like they might be getting ready to ... god knows what ... sabotage a dam, oil fields, something like that."

"And Jud has slipped into their underground, disappeared off the face of the earth." Allsun's voice could cut glass. "You know, the investigators figure Jud gassed me and Neal. They've tried to reconstruct what he was doing here. They think he came out with the intention of killing Chuck and making it look like an accident. So he creates a diversion ... gets Neal and me out of camp just as Chuck is supposed to arrive. Sets up an accident with the observation cage to reinforce how dangerous it is out here, how easy it would be to get killed by a bear." Allsun thinks of Jud watching over her in the lab trailer, taking her pulse. It makes her skin crawl.

"Give me bears any day," Guy says, finishing what's left of Neal's bottle of Glenfiddich. "You know, Jud's father got him the job out here."

Conrad cannot see Allsun, but he has heard the shiver in her voice. He decides it's time they moved on, leave Jud behind. There's still Neal's rivalry to deal with. "So, Neal, what's this CapSeek business you've roped Allsun into?"

"It'll be great. Wade through the swamps. Beat up on a few 'gators and cottonmouth snakes. Nothing like a boondoggle in the deep South." Neal is clearly having fun not answering Conrad's question.

"This is what you call work?" Conrad lets a note of dismissal color his words. "Good thing oil prices are high."

"Don't get me wrong. This is serious shit ... a biological solution to a technological problem."

"Oh, yeah?" Conrad maintains his tone.

Allsun is not amused by the tenor of this game of twenty questions. "Dogs trained to find pin-hole leaks in pipelines buried under mud, water, concrete, anything. CapSeek is the chemical that's put in the pipeline, leaks out and is picked up by the dogs. Right. Now that's settled, Neal, I want you to know I'm not wading through stinking water and mud with cameras around my neck."

"Okay, okay. We'll work something out."

"Over breakfast," Guy interjects. "Time I had my beauty sleep."

"You looked in a mirror lately?" Neal teases.

Guy snores.

ALLSUN AWAKENS WITH a start. She strains to identify what has got her heart beating in her ears. The sound of hissing. God, from where?

Leaping up, she tries to get her bearings in the dark. The propane furnace . . . which corner is it in?

Huffing, she's hearing huffing now. From outside. She opens the Tundra Buggy door a crack and listens. Scuffling below the deck.

Outside, she ventures over to the deck railing. Below are two bears pretending to be pugilists. Circling, punching, holding . . . their white shapes throw up fantastical shadows, polar bears of mythic proportions, polar bears of the Plasticine era. She smiles, remembering.

Allsun has forgotten the cold until Neal comes up behind her and puts a jacket over her shoulders.

"A few friendly rounds," Neal says. "Keeps them in shape for the real thing."

The real thing—males fighting over females for the right to mate. The right to perpetuate themselves, to be saved from oblivion. When she left the Cape last year, Allsun had made up her mind to give Damon that right. This time it was the female fighting for the male. Allsun had made legal application to have Damon's sperm harvested so she could be impregnated. His family thought it an unnatural request and would not give their support. After a year, a judicial decision still had not been reached and Damon had spent yet another twelve months on life support.

"Allsun, just before I left Calgary, Mr. Pythias came to see me. They're worried about you, Al, Damon's family."

"They shouldn't be. I've made the right decision."

"What decision?"

"Did I ever tell you about Damon's name? How his parents named him after a legend without even knowing it? Damon and Pythias were inseparable friends. They lived in Greece sometime during the 4th century B.C. Pythias was condemned to death by the tyrant Dionysius, but was allowed to go home to see his family before his execution, on one condition ... Damon was to agree to take his place and would be executed if Pythias didn't return. The day of the execution, Pythias didn't arrive and Damon was led out to a ring to be gored to death by a bull. Pythias came just in time to save Damon. He had been delayed. He had not abandoned his friend. Dionysius was so struck with this honorable friendship that he pardoned them both. Damon and Pythias became the standard for self-sacrifice."

"Nice story, Al. But you haven't answered my question."

"Damon has a future. Believe me."

Postscript

Keith Rawlings and Bishop Robidoux died in November 1986, when their plane crashed at Rankin Inlet, Northwest Territories.

Polar bear expert Dr. Malcolm Ramsay died May 21, 2000, while returning from tagging polar bears on Lowther Island, west of Resolute, Nunavut, when the helicopter he was a passenger in crashed.